E
21
22
B
OC

LALLIE

LALLIE

Katrina Wright

WORCESTERSHIRE COUNTY COUNCIL
CULTURAL SERVICES

CHIVERS

British Library Cataloguing in Publication Data available

This Large Print edition published by AudioGO Ltd, Bath, 2013.
Published by arrangement with the Author

U.K. Hardcover   ISBN   978 1 4713 2027 9
U.K. Softcover   ISBN   978 1 4713 2028 6

WORCESTERSHIRE COUNTY COUNCIL	
959	
AudioGO	21.06.13
	£16.49
TE	

Printed and bound in Great Britain by
MPG Books Group Limited

To Pam, a dear and valued friend, with love

ONE

Hannah sat in the comfort of the First Class railway carriage as the train chugged northwards, surveying her travelling companions and trying to come to some sort of conclusion about them. Nanny was sprawled in a corner, her mouth open as she slept, and Lallie was quietly watching the scenery slip by through the window. She appeared to be a model child, although Hannah could not help feeling still that there was something unnatural about the girl's tense posture and the erectness with which she held her thin body beneath the expensive travelling coat.

'Are you all right, Lallie?' she asked, leaning forward, and the two sharp brown eyes that fixed themselves unblinkingly on her face gave her, as always when Lallie looked directly at her, a momentary pang of disquiet.

'Yes, thank you, Miss Smith,' Lallie answered composedly. 'I have made this journey before, you know.'

'With your Papa?' enquired Hannah, trying to open some form of communication with the child, who had so far proved unresponsive to her overtures of friendliness.

'Yes—and Nanny and my governesses,' answered Lallie. Then she leaned forward and whispered conspiratorially: 'But none of the

1

governesses liked the house. It's haunted, you know.'

'Haunted?' echoed Hannah, and Lallie nodded vigorously.

'Oh, yes,' she assured Hannah, and added in a mystical voice, her eyes wandering round the carriage in mock-terror: 'There are unquiet spirits, and they manifest themselves. If you see them, they might send you mad.'

Hannah could not repress a smile at the girl's obvious attempt to reduce her to a gibbering wreck.

'Well, it's rather unfortunate, but I don't believe in ghosts,' she said lightly. 'What form do these—er—spirits take? Is there a Grey Lady? Or a Wailing Monk? Or do they simply moan and rattle chains?'

Lallie regarded her solemnly.

'Oh, no, nothing like that. You'll see, Miss Smith. I hope they won't send *you* mad,' she added, in apparent earnestness.

'I don't think that's very likely,' Hannah declared vigorously, and the girl gave her a pitying look before she leaned back into her corner again, and continued to stare out of the window.

Hannah rested her cramped limbs against the plush seat, and recalled the events that had led up to her present situation, trying to fit them in with Lallie's current attempt to frighten her. The visit to the tall, narrow house in Belgravia, where Mr Armstrong had received her alone in a gloomy library.

She had taken an immediate and quite unjustified dislike to the tall, swarthy man with his firm mouth and deep brown eyes, which had flickered expressionlessly over her neat figure in black skirt and white blouse, with a straw boater perched decorously on her coils of fair hair.

'Miss Smith?' He was obviously not a man who believed in wasting words.

'Yes, sir,' she had answered calmly, and he paced the Turkish carpet, hands behind his back, as he said: 'You were recommended to me by Mrs Dobson. I understand you have taught her daughters for some years.'

'Yes, indeed, sir. But now they are going to school,' answered Hannah, thinking with affection of Martha and Matilda and their boisterous excitement at the prospect of school, their genuine sorrow at parting with her.

'So I believe. And you, I presume, are free to accept another post,' Mr Armstrong went on. 'Well, Miss Smith, I have one to offer you, I am a widower—my wife died some ten years ago—and I have a daughter, Lalage.' He paused, then continued: 'My former wife's family home, which I inherited from her, is in North Wales, and it is necessary for me to leave to travel there within a few days to see to business matters regarding the estate. I wish Lalage to join me in a week or so, but

3

at present, she has only her old nurse—my wife's former Nanny—as a companion, and for the two of them to undertake the journey unaccompanied is out of the question. Therefore I find myself obliged to engage a governess for Lalage, one who can supervise her activities and be responsible for her journey both then and thereafter. You are fully qualified? Mrs Dobson gave you the highest recommendation.'

Hannah inclined her head.

'I could, of course, perform these tasks to your satisfaction, I am sure, sir,' she said, then asked: 'May I enquire the age of your daughter?'

'She's thirteen,' he answered shortly.

'But surely,' Hannah protested in bewilderment, 'she has not reached the age of thirteen without some form of tuition? Has she not a governess already?'

He sighed, looking down at the carpet, then up at her.

'We have had governesses by the dozen, Miss Smith. They never stay long. The last one left a month ago.'

'Could you give me some indication why, sir?' asked Hannah, adding quickly: 'It might assist me in my task, if I were to accept the position. Is your daughter a difficult child?'

'No,' said Mr Armstrong, his jaw clenching. 'She obeys me in all respects. Foolish women—claim they can't cope—just hysterical rubbish. Lalage has been brought up to know her duty and to accept authority. There is nothing difficult about her. She's remarkably intelligent for her age.'

Hannah was silent, her gaze wandering round the gloomy room and the unpleasant man in it. Suddenly, she felt sorry for Lalage Armstrong, with no mother, and a father who was obviously a tyrant. This whole house, silent and bleak as the grave, for all its luxury, was no place for a lively thirteen-year-old.

'Might I see Lalage?' she asked, at length, and he replied:

'Certainly. I'll have her summoned.'

Hannah waited as he rang the bell, spoke to a servant and, presently, Lallie herself entered the room. She was a thin, nervous-looking child with long brown hair swept back from her face by a ribbon, and her father's dark eyes. Hannah noted that her white pinafore dress was expensive in design and material, but her heart melted as she saw how it hung on the girl's sparrow-like figure. Why, the child was nothing but a bag of bones.

'Say Good Morning to Miss Smith, Lalage,' commanded Mr Armstrong. 'She will, I hope, be taking the position left by Miss Edge as your governess.'

The girl held out a self-possessed hand.

'Good Morning, Miss Smith,' she repeated obediently, and Hannah took the thin fingers.

'Good Morning, Lalage. I'd like us to be

5

friends,' she said, with a warm smile. The girl did not smile back. Instead, she looked at her father, as though for instructions, and he gave a wave of dismissal.

'That will do.'

Lallie disappeared again, and Mr Armstrong resumed his pacing, staring at Hannah with his black brows drawn together.

'Well? Now you have seen her. You can see that there is nothing wrong with her. May I take it that you will accept the position?'

Hannah thought of the over-large brown eyes, the thin little body.

'Yes, sir,' she said firmly.

'I should be obliged if you could commence your duties tomorrow, if that will be convenient,' Mr Armstrong told her wearily, as though a heavy weight lay on his shoulders. He named a generous salary. At least he was not penny-pinching with his employees, Hannah thought—but probably he had to pay good wages in order to get anyone to work in such a dreary household and for such an unsympathetic master.

He continued: 'I shall leave, as I believe I mentioned, within a few days. I wish you to accompany my daughter to North Wales at the end of the week. I will see to the arrangements for travelling.'

He paused, and turned away as though the conversation was at an end. Hannah waited, but he flicked over the pages of a book that

6

was lying on a table, and appeared to have lost interest in her.

'Surely you wish to give me further instructions, sir,' she ventured, as the pause became uncomfortable, and the dark eyes glanced up at her disinterestedly.

'I leave the child entirely in your hands,' Mr Armstrong stated. 'You may assume absolute authority for her. Teach her if you wish, discipline her if necessary. I would like to make it clear, Miss Smith, that I do not wish to be bothered by petty trivialities. That, I think, is all.'

'Thank you, sir,' said Hannah, and, when he made no move to say goodbye or give her any further orders, she turned quietly and left the room, a wave of dislike for the cold, hard man who could so casually hand his daughter into the care of a stranger, sweeping over her.

Outside, the butler was waiting with her coat, and in a few moments, she was breathing the fresh air of the early summer morning. Ladies in fashionable dress brushed past her as she stood there outside the house, recovering her spirits, which had been slightly dampened by her encounter in the gloomy library. She wondered for a moment why Mr Armstrong— an eligible widower who could surely not be older than his mid-thirties—had never married again, why he was going to North Wales and avoiding the social season, which would give him plenty of opportunity to find another wife.

He must be very rich, and there was certainly nothing wrong with his looks, if one felt attracted to dark, saturnine males. But, as she thought of his unsmiling face, the cold expression in his brown eyes, his casual treatment of his daughter, and his indifference towards herself, she came to the conclusion that Mr Gervaise Armstrong was by nature unsociable. She wondered how he had behaved towards his wife—and decided that if he had been so cold and gloomy towards his young bride, it was no wonder that the poor creature had died.

Still, her business was with Mr Armstrong's daughter, and she did not anticipate that she would have very much to do with the father. He had made it clear that he did not want to be bothered with either Lallie or Hannah, and she certainly could not foresee invitations to dine with him or spend a sociable evening playing the piano in his company. No, her work lay with the child, and, as she thought of Lallie, she realised that she might have some difficulty. Why, for instance, had all the other governesses left?

Hysterical, he had called them. Said they were unable to cope. Hannah squared her shoulders. She determined there and then that *she* would never go sniffing to him and complain that a thirteen-year-old girl was too much for her.

The following morning, she said her

goodbyes to Martha and Matilda and Mrs Dobson, and moved into the tall, dark house. Within a week, Mr Armstrong left for North Wales and, a few days later, she followed him with Lallie and Nanny.

*   *   *

She did not speak to Mr Armstrong again before he left. She was shown her quarters—next to Lallie's—by the housekeeper, and instructed to keep to them unless she wished to take her charge out for a walk, in which case they were to use the back stairs. Her meals were shared with the child in the schoolroom, and her evenings spent reading or writing letters in her room after Lallie had gone to bed. If she wished to go out of the house, said Mrs Buxton, the housekeeper, she must use the servants' door.

At least Mrs Buxton was tentatively friendly, and tried to make sure Hannah was comfortable, but when Hannah attempted to draw her out on the subject of her employer, she set her mouth primly and declared:

'He goes his own way, miss, and none of us interfere. That's the way it's always been since the mistress died. Yes, I suppose the house *is* a bit gloomy, but we're snug enough in the Servants' Hall, and so long as we do our work properly, he never complains. You'd scarcely know he was here, half the time.'

9

She refused, however, to be drawn into further gossip, saying she had work to do, and rustled off with her bunch of keys clinking at her ample waist.

Tentatively, Hannah questioned Lallie.

'Does your Papa never come up to see you? Does he never send for you in the evenings to join him in the drawing-room?'

Lallie shrugged.

'No,' she said briefly, and Hannah felt her heart go out to this neglected child, while her indignation at Mr Armstrong's treatment of his daughter swelled accordingly. She turned to Lallie with renewed vigour, in an attempt to make up for what the child lacked in love and affection.

Lallie answered any questions she asked, but rarely spoke unless spoken to, and spent her time largely with her sketch-pad and pencils, wrapped in a world of her own. Hannah asked if she could see the drawings, but the child shut the book with a defiant air.

'I never show my drawings to *anybody*. Not even Nanny.'

'Well, never mind,' said Hannah cheerfully, and suggested that she might give Lallie a lesson in history.

She discovered, during their few days in London, that the girl was bright and quick, with a lively intelligence, and very much advanced in lessons for her age.

'I don't think I need to worry too much

10

about teaching you for a while, until we have got to know each other better,' Hannah said brightly. 'So when we go to North Wales, I think we'll make it a holiday, at least for the first few weeks. Shall you like that?'

Again, Lallie shrugged. It seemed to be her reaction to everything.

On her first day in the Armstrong household, Hannah had met Nanny, and she regarded the elderly woman with some slight trepidation, wondering whether Nanny would resent her. But the plump, elderly woman with her neat black dress and grey hair pulled back from her face, seemed to be friendly, and to accept her, as Lallie herself had done. Hannah soon discovered, however, that Nanny was devoted to the child, and spoiled her outrageously, making no attempt to control or discipline her. Hannah wasn't sure whether this was a good thing, and wondered whether Nanny would resent her own authority over the child—for she intended to establish her position, though making sure that Lallie understood that her new governess had her interests at heart. Children responded well to a certain amount of discipline and a regular routine, Hannah had discovered, and she was already making plans to organize Lallie's time and not let the girl do whatever she pleased, whenever she felt like it.

Once, going downstairs on an errand to the kitchen, Hannah crept into the hall, drawn by the sound of voices. She could hear Mr Armstrong's emotionless, measured tones, and to her indignation, the words, which she could not make out, were followed by the sound of a stifled sob. So he bullied the servants, did he? No doubt for some trifling blunder, she thought with a surge of anger, for some mistake or oversight. Movements in the room sent her scurrying on her way to the servants' quarters, but she did not forget the little incident.

She decided that the house was a most unhappy place, and was glad they would be leaving soon, although of course, Mr Armstrong would be present on their holiday in North Wales. But Hannah hoped fervently that business would keep him busy, and they would not see much of him. An event during the night before their departure only served to intensify her conviction that this atmosphere of gloom was not a suitable place for a child.

She had fallen asleep, but was awakened in the early hours of the morning by a noise which she realized after a moment was coming from Lallie's room, next to her own. It sounded like a series of gasps. Hannah immediately lit the lamp, put on her robe, and went through to the child.

She found Lallie curled up with her face buried in the pillow, her dark hair damp with perspiration, and her eyes wild. She was sobbing, but obviously trying to hide her distress.

'Lallie dear, whatever is it?' said Hannah gently, setting down the lamp and sitting beside the girl, trying to put her arms round the trembling figure, but, with a heroic effort, Lallie gulped down her sobs, and said in a sullen tone:

'Nothing. Go away.'

'Did you have a nightmare?' probed Hannah, thinking that it was not surprising if the poor child did suffer from night fears in a house like this.

'No,' Lallie answered defiantly, and pushed Hannah's arm away.

'Then why are you crying, darling?' Hannah asked, but Lallie only stared at her coldly, the tears still in her eyes, and repeated:

'I'm all right. Go away.'

Hannah had enough experience with children to realize that the girl regarded her as an interloper, and would not admit her secret fears, whatever they were. She preferred to try and fight them herself rather than accept sympathy, and Hannah would only do further harm if she attempted to force the child to accept her comfort.

She rose from the bed.

'Very well, dear,' she said calmly. 'If you're sure you're all right. Would you like me to leave the lamp for you?'

'No,' snapped Lallie, and Hannah picked it up.

13

'As you wish. But if you want me, you have only to call, and I'll come. I'm not far away, you know.' She paused, but the defiant little face did not change, so she said briskly: 'Well, then, I'll see you in the morning, dear.'

And she went back to her own room, where she sat on the edge of the bed, her forehead puckered into a frown. She was going to have to be very patient and edge her way gently into the child's confidence.

But she was determined to try, and not to be put off. She was sure Lallie needed help and love, and Hannah could not resist a child in need. There and then, she made up her mind that she would do everything in her power to befriend the girl, discover what secret unhappiness made her cry in the night, and try to cure her of her fears.

*   *   *

They left for the railway station the next day, and Lallie appeared to have recovered her spirits and seemed to be looking forward to the journey. Hannah herself was in a gay mood. It was a lovely day, and they were setting out for the country, where there would be fields and trees.

The carriage arrived, and with Mrs Buxton looking on, Lallie scrambled in, to be followed by a wheezing Nanny, and finally, Hannah. Their luggage was safely stowed, and the

14

driver whipped up the horses. Mrs Buxton waved, and Hannah waved back.

Then there was the excitement of the railway station, as they began their journey north. They were on their way. The city gave place to the greenery Hannah had visualized, and she gave herself up to the pleasure of watching the passing scenery, the little houses, the cows and horses, the birds, the sunny sky. Nanny dozed, but Lallie too seemed to take a delight in watching the scenery—at least at first.

As the journey progressed, Lallie began to make random remarks without being prompted, and although they were mostly of a discouraging nature ('You might not like the house, Miss Smith, it has no modern facilities at all'), Hannah felt that her pupil's attitude was a sign for the good. She encouraged Lallie by taking up her comments.

'Tell me more about it,' she said brightly. 'What is it called, for instance?'

'Bethel House,' Lallie answered, and volunteered: 'That's because the little village nearby is called Bethel. Actually, in Wales, Bethel is usually the name of a chapel.'

'I expect you know quite a lot about Wales, having been there a lot,' smiled Hannah, and Lallie shrugged.

'Not really.'

'Your Mama was Welsh, I believe?' said Hannah, with genuine interest. 'I understand

15

that this was her family home. Are her own Mama and Papa still there?'

Lallie shook her head.

'No, they're dead.'

'Dead?' repeated Hannah. Surely, she thought, they could not have been very old.

'They died in some sort of accident—I don't know much about it. I think a wheel came off a gig or a trap when they were going very fast, and they were thrown out and killed,' said Lallie, losing interest. 'The house is kept shut up now unless Papa or I—and Nanny and my governess—go there. A housekeeper looks after it with her husband—he's a sort of handyman. Mr and Mrs Jones. You'll meet them. When we go, they engage temporary help from the villages and farms round about.'

She stared pointedly out of the window, and Hannah sat back. At least she was making a little progress. It was later when Lallie made her startling pronouncement about the house being haunted, and, by then, they were a long way on their journey. Hannah was feeling sticky and dusty, but she had no time to bother about her looks, for there was the necessity of changing trains to catch the little local train that would take them to the nearest station to Bethel.

They had long ago eaten their picnic luncheon, and Hannah hoped that Bethel was not too far. The scenery was becoming wilder and more beautiful, and she gazed with

16

wonder and delight at the green fields and hills, and the chain of mountains that rose in the west, like crouching monsters against the sunset. At last, they chugged into the tiny station, and Lallie informed her that they had arrived. Nanny woke and looked round her with satisfaction.

'And about time, too,' she said.

'I hope that Mr Jones has brought the carriage to meet us,' said Lallie, as they commenced the operation of descending from the train with their luggage.

'So do I,' said Nanny, yawning widely, although she had in fact slept for most of the journey. 'I'm that tired. Something to eat and a soft bed, that's what my old bones need.'

The station master fussed round their baggage, and Hannah had her first experience of hearing the Welsh language spoken, a soft, lilting sound. Then Lallie ran across the little platform, waving.

'Mr Jones! Mr Jones, here we are,' she called.

In the gathering dusk of the early summer night, they were ushered by Mr Jones, who proved to be a plump, cheery man, into the waiting carriage, and their boxes and bags were piled up on the top. Then the horse set off through the sweet scents of the country, where Hannah could see tangles of wild flowers and tall grass in the hedgerows. She leaned out eagerly, as they made their way along narrow, twisting lanes. Soon they came to a wide and beautiful river.

'We're nearly there,' Lallie volunteered to Hannah. 'We just have to cross the bridge, and the house is straight ahead.'

'You mean it stands on the river bank?' queried Hannah, intrigued, and Lallie answered:

'Well, not exactly on the bank. But the lawn slopes down to the bank. I fish there sometimes, but I always put the fish back.' She added, as though speaking her thoughts aloud: 'I think it's cruel to kill anything.'

A moment later, the carriage turned across the arch of a stony bridge, and Lallie pointed out of the carriage window.

'There we are, Miss Smith.'

Hannah peered out. In the dusk, the house rose, tall and stately, with what appeared to be a battlemented roof, and a large number of chimneys. Lights were flickering in some of the windows, and as the carriage turned into the short drive and pulled up before the front door, Hannah saw a porch with stone pillars, and steps. The door was open, and figures were outlined against the warm glow from within.

'There's Papa. And Mrs Jones, waiting for us,' said Lallie, and was the first to scramble down when the step was lowered. Nanny followed her, and then Hannah stepped down, holding up her long skirt with one hand.

18

'Good evening, Papa,' Lallie said dutifully, bobbing a little curtsey, and Mr Armstrong folded his arms.

'Good evening, Lalage. Nanny. Miss Smith. You had a passably pleasant journey, I hope?'

'Yes, sir, I think we have managed to get here with all our possessions safe and sound,' Hannah replied, and added impulsively: 'I did not imagine the house would be so—so impressive—and set in such beautiful countryside—'

He cut her short.

'I did not build the house, Miss Smith. I cannot take the responsibility for its "impressiveness", nor indeed for the countryside,' he said coldly. 'Mrs Jones will see to your needs. I have already dined, and I have work to do, so I will bid you all good night.'

And with that, he turned and disappeared into the hall. Hannah felt herself flushing indignantly. She felt as though he had slapped her face. What a really unpleasant man he was!

They were left with the small, neat figure of the housekeeper, on whom Lallie advanced with outstretched hand.

'Good evening, Mrs Jones,' she said, in the tones of a duchess, and Mrs Jones smiled a welcome.

'Well, Miss Lallie. So here you are again, is it? And Nanny—how are you, Nanny?—and who's this?' She peered at Hannah.

19

'This is my new governess, Miss Smith,' Lallie said regally. 'I hope you've got a room ready for her too. The gold room, I think.'

There was a silence, which made itself felt even though Mr Jones was engaged in unloading the luggage.

Then Mrs Jones said, rather disapprovingly, Hannah thought:

'If you say so, miss.'

'I do,' said Lallie, and there was something in her tone which made Hannah look at her sharply, but the girl's face was a picture of innocence.

The inside of the house was just as elaborate as Hannah had expected. A great hall tiled in black and white had a staircase leading up on the left which made a sharp turn and became a long gallery that stretched across the length of the hall, with doors leading off it. Mr Jones started up the stairs with the baggage, while Mrs Jones, who quite obviously did what Lallie told her, threw open one of the downstairs doors and ushered them into an enormous drawing-room, decorated in the early Victorian style, with elegant, but shabby furniture. A huge fire was burning, though the night was warm.

'Would you like to see your room first, Miss Smith, or freshen up, or have something to eat?' Mrs Jones asked rather nervously, and Hannah smiled at her.

'I feel rather grimy, but I'd prefer to eat, if

20

it's not too much trouble. We had luncheon a long time ago.'

'No trouble. I thought you'd all be hungry,' said Mrs Jones. 'Perhaps Miss Lallie would just show you where to wash your hands,' and she disappeared through another door at the far end of the room.

'This way, Miss Smith,' said Lallie, and led Hannah out into the hall and along a corridor. 'Here's the downstairs cloakroom and bathroom. I told you this house is very antiquated.'

Hannah thanked her, and went into an ornate Victorian room with bathroom furnishings that caused her to smile and imagine how many gallons of water would be necessary to fill the enormous bath. She washed her hands, splashed her face, and, feeling distinctly fresher, emerged to where Lallie was waiting.

'Now your turn. Clean hands for dinner, please,' Hannah said, and Lallie shrugged and disappeared. Hannah heard the sound of water sloshing about in the wash-stand, and in a few seconds, Lallie came out, looking virtuous. She led the way back to the drawing-room.

They had both taken off their coats, and Hannah carefully removed her hat. The room was very hot. Nanny was sunk into the embrace of a brocaded sofa as though she was exhausted.

'Well, Miss Smith?' asked Lallie

challengingly. 'What do you think of it?'

'From what I've seen, it's very beautiful—and unusual,' said Hannah. 'Lallie, why did you ask for me to have the—er—gold room? That sounds as though it was meant for important visitors.'

'Why, it's next to mine, and I wouldn't want to be too far away from you, would I, Miss Smith?' Lallie answered composedly, looking Hannah unblinkingly in the eyes. 'It's only called the gold room because of the colour of the draperies, that's all. I thought you'd like it. It looks out over the river and the mountains.'

'Well, that was very thoughtful of you, dear,' Hannah said warmly, and an expression of—could it be smugness?—passed fleetingly across Lallie's face.

Then Mrs Jones came in to tell them that dinner was about to be served in the dining-room. This proved to be next to the drawing-room, and was furnished with an enormous table and its accompanying chairs. At the side of the room stood a magnificent Victorian sideboard, heavily carved from polished dark wood.

Mrs Jones had a young girl waiting to serve them, whom she introduced as Angharad, and who was obviously not used to waiting at table. But she managed valiantly, and the chicken soup, roast beef and vegetables, and cherry pie and cream were delicious. When they had finished, and were drinking coffee, Hannah had begun to feel quite sleepy, while Nanny was yawning prodigiously.

'Thank you, Mrs Jones, that was superb,' Hannah said, as they rose. 'Now, Lallie, Nanny is tired, so am I, we've had a long day and it's past your bed-time. I suggest we all get to bed as soon as possible.'

'The gold room is ready, Miss Lallie,' interposed Mrs Jones, casting a speculative look at Hannah.

'I'll show it to you, shall I?' Lallie asked her governess, and Hannah was touched by the girl's apparent anxiety that she should be comfortable.

'If you wish, dear,' she said, as the general move was made towards the stairs. They climbed up to the first floor, and Lallie led Hannah along the gallery and down another corridor.

'This is Nanny's room,' she said, indicating a door. 'And this is one of the upstairs bathrooms—there are two—' Moving on. 'I'm afraid we all have to share the same bathroom on this side of the house. I told you there is no gas or any modern facilities here. If you want hot water, the girls will have to bring it up from the kitchen. Here is my room, and yours is next door—here we are—it's at the corner of the house.'

'Where does your Papa sleep?' Hannah could not help asking curiously, and Lallie shrugged.

'On the other side of the house. And he has a study downstairs which nobody is ever allowed to go into. We don't see him very much.'

'I suppose he's—busy with estate business,' Hannah said thoughtfully, and Lallie said carelessly:

'I don't know. But he does a lot of working in his study. Now let me show you your room.'

She opened the door in question, and Hannah, who was carrying a candelabra with five candles, went through into a pleasant and elegant chamber, decorated in autumn colours, with gold-tinted drapes that were closed across the windows that took up almost two of the walls.

'Why, it's charming,' Hannah said, setting down the candelabra. Her boxes, she noticed, had been placed at the foot of the bed, and there was water in the washstand, with soap and a towel. 'I'm sure I shall be comfortable here, Lallie dear. Would you like me to see you to bed before I settle down?'

'It's all right, I can manage,' Lallie said offhandedly, and Hannah smiled warmly.

'Well, then, goodnight, darling. Have a good sleep and pleasant dreams. Don't forget that if you want me, I'll come.'

'I'll be all right. I hope you have a good night too, Miss Smith,' said Lallie, and she moved away down the corridor carrying her own candle in its flowered china holder.

Hannah was unpacking her nightgown and robe when there was a knock on the door. She opened it and, to her amazement, Mr Armstrong stood there, the candle he was holding throwing flickering shadows across his dark face.

'I instructed Mrs Jones to prepare the red room for you,' he said abruptly. 'But I understand Lalage has insisted you should have this one.'

'It seems—very pleasant, sir. I hope you are not displeased,' Hannah faltered, for he was frowning.

'No—no. Except that—' He paused, then said with an effort. 'I apologize for my boorish behaviour when you arrived, Miss Smith. I was—rather busy.'

'I understand, sir,' Hannah said coldly.

'I hope you will be comfortable here,' he continued, and hesitated, as though he was going to say something else, then seemed to change his mind, and merely added: 'Goodnight, Miss Smith.'

'Goodnight, sir,' she answered, and he withdrew without further ado, leaving Hannah bewildered. How strange of him to come, in most uncharacteristic fashion, to make sure she was properly settled. And to actually apologize for his behaviour! She felt as though she had scored some sort of triumph, and it was with a pleasant feeling of elation tingling through her veins that she washed her face and hands and prepared for bed. She was very tired, and cramped from so much travelling. She was certain she would sleep like a log in the comfortable bed.

Once she had extinguished her candles, she lay in the warmth, listening to the quiet of the countryside. Everywhere was very still. It reminded her of her own childhood in the little village in Devon, before her family had moved to London, but she had forgotten just how disconcerting such absolute silence could be, with only the small, murmuring sounds of the night. But all the same, it was not long before she was asleep.

*   *   *

She awoke suddenly with a start. Surely there was something wrong. It took a moment for her senses to become adjusted, then she realized that there was a noise coming from her window, a knocking and rattling on the glass. Her heart began to beat quickly as she recalled Lallie's words that the house was haunted, but she told herself firmly that she did not believe in such nonsense.

Her hands were shaking, however, as she quickly lit the candles—noting that there was no lamp in the room—and went across to the window. The knocking had stopped, but it took all Hannah's courage to fling back the curtain. The window glass reflected her image and the flickering flames of the candelabra, but nothing else. There was nothing there.

Hannah took a deep breath as she let the curtain fall back into place. She must have been dreaming, and imagined the noise. But nevertheless, she decided to leave the candles burning, at least until her panic had subsided, and she set the candelabra down while she poured herself a drink of water, and sat on the bed to sip it slowly. The room seemed as pleasant and peaceful as ever.

Then her head jerked upright. There was no draught, the flames were burning straight and tall, but, one by one, even as she watched, they seemed to wither and die. Shadows filled the room. One candle went out—then another. Just before the last one disappeared, Hannah had seized the box of lucifer matches and tried to relight them, but they would not light. She was alone in the dark.

With a quickened breath, and her heart pumping loudly beneath her nightdress, she waited, but still there was absolute silence in the rest of the house. She felt very uneasy— and at a complete loss to explain what had happened. She did not believe in ghosts—yet what had caused her candles to go out?

Reluctant to wander the unfamiliar corridors in the dark, she decided that the best thing she could do was to get back into bed and try to sleep until the morning, when perhaps she could solve the mystery. So she crept between the sheets, and pulled them up tightly round her neck. She lay stiffly and waited, but nothing else happened, and, after a long time, she fell into an uneasy doze. When she woke, dawn was breaking, and she could see chinks of light from behind the closed curtains. With deep thankfulness, she realized that the strange, bewildering first night at Bethel House was over.

TWO

The first thing Hannah did was to investigate the two odd happenings during the night. In the pearly dawn, with the misty sun rising, she drew back the window drapes and inspected the windows. They were the type that opened with a catch, and she opened one and leaned out, breathing in the fresh morning air.

There was no sign of ivy or any climbing plant which could have caused the tapping on the window. But a little further along was the window of Lallie's room, and Hannah noted that it was half-open. If Lallie had leaned out—

Thoughtfully, remembering the girl's obvious attempts to frighten her in the last few days, she rummaged through her luggage for her parasol, and, leaning out of the window, measured the distance to Lallie's

28

room. It reached easily. Nanny's room, much further away, was quite out of reach, and Mr Armstrong slept on the other side of the house, so they could have had nothing to do with the tapping. Hannah withdrew her parasol, and put it down, her mind clicking over the facts.

Lallie had told her the house was haunted— and it must have been Lallie who had leaned out and tapped on her window with a parasol or umbrella. Hannah could only conclude that Lallie took delight in frightening every governess who was employed by her father away, and fully expected Hannah to follow her predecessors. She decided that the best thing she could do was to ignore the tapping and say nothing about it, until she could get to know the child better.

But the candles were a different matter. Hannah examined them carefully. She could not be sure, but it seemed to her that the wicks had been broken or cut, possibly by inserting a needle, or something of the sort part of the way down the wax, so that when they burned down to the severed part, they would automatically go out. But Lallie had been in her view all the previous evening, and she could not possibly have tampered with the candles. She had not left Hannah's side.

Then someone else must have done it. Nanny? Hannah did not think so, for Nanny had collapsed into the settee in the drawing-room, and had been with them all the time during the dinner. Yet someone must have touched her candles—someone who knew where they were waiting, lined up on a chest at the bottom of the stairs, someone who knew Hannah would be given the candelabra.

She supposed that Mr or Mrs Jones or one of the other servants might have been responsible, but why should they? They had never seen Hannah before that evening. They did not know her.

That left only one person—Mr Armstrong, and as she thought about him, Hannah frowned. He would certainly have had the opportunity while they were at dinner, and it may even have been he who, as master of the house, had decreed that Hannah should have the candelabra. Then there was his strange visit to her room after they had retired for the night. It did not seem characteristic of the cold, hard man she imagined him to be. He had seemed—well, almost hesitant, too, as though there was something he wished to say to her, but had then changed his mind. Hannah decided that she could not rule him out, although she could not imagine what his motive might be.

It was all very odd, and she could make no sense of it. She decided that, even though it was scarcely six o'clock and the rest of the house was still asleep, she would go out for a walk and try to clear her mind of the bewildering events of the night.

She dressed carefully, and went along the corridor past the closed doors of Lallic's and Nanny's rooms, then along the gallery and down into the hall. No doubt there was another more convenient door they could use to go in and out of the house, but she did not know where it was, so she pulled back the bolts of the front door, and turned the huge key—which was fortunately still in the lock—and stepped outside into the morning, pulling the door behind her.

The prospect from the front of the house was absolutely beautiful. On the left, the river ran smoothly, crystal-clear, and as Lallie had promised, the lawn swept down to the very edge of its banks. She could see the stone bridge they had crossed last night a little further away, and beyond, on every side, green hills, with a towering peak of amethyst in the distance. Wales was lovely, Hannah thought, as she began to walk briskly towards the bridge.

She could see signs of habitation amid trees on the far bank, about half-a-mile away, and she thought she would peep at the village before the occupants were astir, though already, thin columns of smoke were ascending from cottage fires. But Hannah was a friendly person, and even if the people could not speak English, she considered that a smile could break any language barrier.

31

She had crossed the bridge, and was walking along a narrow lane between tall hedgerows, listening to the birds as they sang in the brightening warmth of the sun, when she heard the sound of hooves and wheels behind her, and pulled herself as far to the side of the lane as she could to make room for the approaching vehicle. A trap turned the corner, and when the driver saw her, he clucked to the horse.

'Whoa there! Strawberry!'

The dainty little mare came to a stop, flicking her ears, and the driver leaned down to Hannah.

'Good morning. You're up and about very early.'

'I might say the same about you,' Hannah answered, returning his smile. He was young and fair, with grey eyes and blond hair, but his high cheekbones proclaimed his Welsh ancestry. His voice had a musical lilt to it, and his rugged grin was infectious.

'Ah, but I have an excuse. I've been up all night at a confinement. May I introduce myself? Dr Owen Richards, at your service.'

'A doctor?' Hannah was intrigued, but she hastily remembered her manners. She responded: 'I am Hannah Smith. I'm Lalage Armstrong's new governess. Her father has come to Bethel House for a visit, and Lallie and her Nanny and I have come too. Do you know Mr Armstrong, at all, doctor?'

'Please—call me Owen,' he insisted, with frank admiration in his grey eyes. 'You're not my patient—and I hope you're not going to require my professional services while you are here. Can't we be friends?'

'I'd like that,' said Hannah, before she had had time to consider her words, then she blushed at her temerity, but he tactfully interposed:

'Don't worry about being forward or improper here, Miss Smith. Everybody knows everyone else on first-name terms. It's like that in a village, especially a little one like Bethel. I found it terribly difficult to be formal and correct when I was away at University and Medical School.' He grinned his boyish grin again. 'I was always getting into trouble for rushing up to young ladies and asking them their name, and all about themselves. Many the time I've had my cheek slapped.'

He rubbed his cheek ruefully, and Hannah could not help laughing. It was impossible to dislike this irrepressible Welshman, or to feel uncomfortable in his presence.

'Well, if I am to call you Owen, you will have to call me Hannah,' she said, and he bowed.

'I would consider that a very great honour,' he said, and declared: 'Miss Hannah it shall be.'

'Were you—were you born here in the village?' Hannah asked, turning the subject away from herself, and within a few moments, he was bantering and laughing again as he told her of how he had always wanted to follow in his father's footsteps as a doctor, and the means by which it had been achieved.

'And now—well, Father is dead. I did take over his place, but I wish he could have lived longer,' he said regretfully. 'Mother and I live in that house over there—look, you can just see it behind those trees, with the white chimneys. It's called 'Bodwena', but everyone always refers to it as 'the Doctor's house'.'

'It's beautiful here. You're lucky to live in a place like this always,' Hannah said involuntarily, and he smiled.

'Mr Armstrong could live here always if he wanted to.'

Hannah felt curiosity stealing over her.

'I believe Lalage—Lallie, my pupil—I believe her mother's family home was here at Bethel House. Did you ever know her as a young girl?'

He nodded. 'She was older than me, but I knew her. A sweet, gentle creature, with a tiny waist and huge violet eyes. I understand she died of consumption, not long after her daughter was born.'

'Poor lady! But judging from the way you have described her, the child must take after her father. She has his dark hair and brown eyes,' Hannah mused, half to herself. The doctor was silent, and Hannah was suddenly struck by the weariness in his face.

'You're tired!' she exclaimed, reproaching herself. 'If you've been up all night at a confinement, you must be in need of rest. I'm so sorry. I shouldn't have kept you talking.'

'Not at all. I'm glad we have met,' he smiled, looking into her face so that she flushed. 'Can we meet again, Miss Hannah? Might I call?'

'Please do, Dr Owen,' she answered composedly, re-collecting herself. She had been speaking to him as though he was an old friend—but somehow, she felt almost as though he was.

He said goodbye, clicked his tongue to the little mare, and the trap moved off down the lane, and rounded a corner. Hannah wandered on, enjoying the sensation of a summer morning coming to life around her, and sniffing ecstatically at the sweet air, which she thought was like wine.

She could not help thinking of the gentle girl Dr Owen—and as she recalled his frank admiration and his warm, irresistible smile, the blood surged up into her face again—had described as Lallie's mother, and wondering how Mr Armstrong had treated this sweet creature. Had he been his familiar cold, harsh self, or had he really loved his young bride, and been devastated by her death? Did that, perhaps, explain his aversion to society and his hard manner? Yet Mrs Armstrong had died ten years ago, and ten years was a long time to

35

mourn. Then there was the child. She was Mrs Armstrong's daughter, as well as her father's. Did he not care for Lallie for her mother's sake, that he ignored her and gave her no love?

Pondering on the problem of Mr Armstrong's character reminded Hannah that she had allowed herself to be distracted from the odd events of the previous night .The sooner she could get to grips with who had tampered with her candles, and find out some more about the house and its inhabitants, the better. Determined to begin a subtle campaign to discover who was responsible for the stupid tricks played on her, she retraced her steps and headed back towards the bridge.

*   *   *

To Hannah's surprise, Mr Armstrong joined the rest for breakfast but, though she watched him closely, she could see no evidence that he was wondering whether she had been frightened when her candles went out, leaving her alone in the dark. He seemed preoccupied, and ate in silence, his thoughts obviously elsewhere.

It was Lallie who enquired innocently:

'Did you sleep well, Miss Smith?'

'Yes, indeed,' Hannah replied brightly, certain now that Lallie had been responsible for the rapping on the window, but keeping

36

to her plan not to mention it. 'But something seems to be wrong with the candles in Wales. Mine burned out when I was reading a few pages of Dickens' *Christmas Carol* before settling myself for the night. It was most inconvenient. I think I had better have a lamp in case it happens in the future, Lallie. I'll tell Mrs Jones later.'

Lallie's face became impassive, and she shrugged. 'How about you? No nightmares, I hope—or visits from the ghost you told me about?' smiled Hannah teasingly, and Lallie glanced at her father, her cheeks burning red.

'No,' she said shortly.

'Good. Perhaps the ghost has decided to move elsewhere, since this house is so often closed-up,' Hannah suggested, and Mr Armstrong, who had finished his breakfast, interrupted impassively:

'Pray excuse me, ladies. My work calls me.'

'Certainly, sir,' said Hannah, matching his tone, and they all watched as he strode from the room. Then Nanny, who rarely spoke, leaned forward and said reprovingly:

'It's not wise to mock at the spirits, Miss Smith. This is ancient country. Perhaps you've heard of the Druids?'

'Druids? Weren't they some sort of religious leaders of the people in olden days?' Hannah asked, intrigued.

'Spirits can linger. There's a Druidic Circle on the top of the hill over there,' Nanny informed her, pointing out of the window of the dining-room. 'They gathered to perform their secret rites.'

'And I suppose their ghosts haunt Bethel House? Well, quite honestly, I can't see the connection,' said Hannah, half amused at Nanny's belief in country superstitions. 'After all, so Lallie informs me, this house is protected by a Christian name—the name of a chapel. And why should the old Druids choose this particular house to haunt, anyway?'

'The ghost isn't a Druid, Miss Smith,' Lallie said smugly. 'It's a baby.'

'A what?' Hannah stared at the girl, her fork checked with a piece of kidney half-way to her mouth.

'A baby. It was drowned in the river, and sometimes, you can hear it crying,' said Lallie. 'Especially on rainy nights. You wait until a rainy night, Miss Smith, then you'll hear it for yourself.'

Hannah was silent. What a strange mixture of stories! Not that she believed in any of them—certainly not the ghostly Druids.

'You seem to know a lot about this area, Nanny,' she said, turning to the woman in the dark dress. 'Do you come from around these parts?'

'I was born and bred here—in this very house. My mother was Nanny to the old mistress,' Nanny answered, flushing, and Hannah tried to put her at her ease.

'So you followed on and became Mrs Armstrong's Nanny?' she asked, and the woman's eyes met hers.

'Yes. Miss Caroline was in my care from the day she was born,' she answered, and Hannah was touched to see traces of tears at the corners of her eyes. Nanny wiped them away.

'I'm so sorry. She died young, didn't she?' Hannah said gently, and Nanny cast her a venomous look.

'It was him that drove her to it,' she declared bitterly, and stumbled from the room. Hannah looked at Lallie.

'Does she mean your father?' she asked, slightly shocked, and Lallie shrugged. 'But I thought—I mean, somebody told me—that she died of consumption.'

'I can't remember her. Except that she was always lying on a sofa,' said Lallie. 'Then Papa took her away—Mrs Buxton told me—and she died in Switzerland.'

'He must have taken her there for the air, to try and cure her complaint,' Hannah deduced, but Lallie did not appear to be interested, so she decided to drop the subject.

'Well, it's a beautiful day. What shall we do with ourselves?' she said brightly. 'Are you going to give me a tour of the house, Lallie dear?'

'If you like,' said Lallie indifferently, and they finished their breakfast and rose to leave the dining-room.

39

During the morning, Lallie dutifully conducted Hannah over the many rooms of the house. Most of the bedrooms were shut up, covered with dust-sheets, and Lallie pointed out one door downstairs that was grimly shut.

'That's Papa's study,' she whispered. 'I expect he's in there now, working. He hates to be disturbed.'

They passed on, and came eventually to a room which took Hannah's fascinated attention.

'This is the Mirror Room,' Lallie informed her, turning the door-knob, and Hannah stepped through into a fairy-land. The room was octagonal, and huge mirrors were fixed to every side of the wall, so that she and Lallie were reflected a million times over, and the light, which came in through a dome at the top, was broken into thousands of fragmented sunbeams.

Interspersed with the mirrors were paintings of nymphs, shepherdesses, and merry youths dancing hand in hand, and the room was an absolute delight.

'Why—I can't believe it! How utterly lovely! Surely this wasn't part of the original house?' Hannah said involuntarily.

'No, I think someone built it on later. We call it Elijah's Folly,' said Lallie. She seemed preoccupied, and suddenly she turned to Hannah, her huge brown eyes filled with some indescribable emotion.

'Miss Smith—' she began.

'Yes, dear?' said Hannah, sensing that perhaps she had at last broken through Lallie's reserve. 'What is it?'

'Miss Smith—aren't you afraid of *anything?*' Lallie faltered, not looking at Hannah, but reaching out a much-reflected hand towards one of the mirrors and drawing a shape with her finger on the glass.

Hannah hesitated.

'Well, that's a big question, Lallie dear,' she said at last. 'I don't believe in ghostly Druids, or unquiet spirits. I don't think God would let such things harm me. That's if there are any. You're not afraid of the ghosts, are you?'

Lallie shook her head violently.

'Oh, no.'

'Of course, there are things we all fear,' Hannah went on carefully. 'And the world seems especially frightening when we are young. Is there something special frightening you? Can you tell me what it is? Then perhaps we can get rid of it for you.'

Lallie hesitated, then, with a sudden change of mood, she tossed her head, ran out of the Mirror Room, and taunted: 'You can't catch me!' The door slammed shut behind her.

Hannah bit her lip. She had been almost on the verge of winning the girl's confidence, she was certain, but at the last moment, Lallie had drawn back. And who could blame her? After all, Hannah was still a comparative stranger to her, even though they were slowly getting to know each other. Hannah sighed. She'd just have to keep on trying, for by now she was convinced that Lallie had some secret anxiety, and she was determined to help the child overcome it.

She turned to follow the girl from the room, then stopped, looking around her in bewilderment. The door seemed to have vanished. On every side of her was a mirror, and since the room had no windows, she had lost her sense of direction. She concluded irritably that the door also possessed a mirror—something she had not noticed when she entered—and that when it was shut, the octagonal of shining glass was complete, to baffle the stranger. No wonder they called it a Folly.

But there must surely be a handle. Hannah went carefully round every side of the room, but to her dismay, there was nothing to indicate which piece of glass opened outwards, and the lines of the door had fallen into place with the rest of the panelling that was painted so gaily with nymphs and shepherds. She seemed to be trapped.

'Lallie!' she called, banging on one of the sheets of glass. 'Lallie! the door has shut! Let me out!'

Silence.

'Lallie!' Hannah shouted again, even louder, a stirring of panic beginning to rise within her. Had the child shut her in deliberately?

She realized with a sinking heart that the room must be soundproof—the panelling would muffle any cries from within. No-one would hear her—and Lallie was the only person who knew where she was. No-one else would think of coming to open the door.

Hannah gave a sigh of exasperation. This was ridiculous! She looked up at the glass dome above, trying to gain a sense of direction from the sunlight which streamed in at an angle, but she had not taken note of where the door was in relation to the sun when she came into the room with Lallie, and she eventually had to give up her calculations.

In the centre of the room was a completely round, padded velvet seat, and Hannah sat down on it, her reflection following suit as a hundred Hannahs did the same. She tried to remain calm. Lallie would come back. She could not leave her governess there for ever. This was a civilized house, not some barbarian castle.

But after she had sat for what seemed hours, trying to keep her composure, she was driven to try once again to find the door, and she prowled all round the room, looking for a catch, or a latch, or some indication of which sheet of glass was the door. She tried tapping the panels, but they all sounded the same and, at last, she was forced to give up. It was obvious that unless one knew the secret, the door could only be opened from without. She would just have to wait for Lallie to relent and come to free her.

By this time, she was feeling both hungry and thirsty, and it occurred to her that it was long past luncheon. She felt tired, dishevelled and dispirited, as she sank down once again onto the padded seat. She had been so close to gaining Lallie's confidence, and now the child had done this to her. Why?

Suddenly, her commonsense gave her the reason. They had just been talking about fear, and Lallie had been about to confide her anxiety. But the child must have a deep distrust of all adults. Hannah would have to prove herself in order to win Lallie's complete trust, and no doubt this was another of the girl's methods of testing Hannah's nerve.

She could picture other governesses—the ones who had not stayed—being driven into hysterics by the little tricks that had been played upon her since they arrived—the tapping on the window—the candles going out—and now being shut into a room from which she was powerless to escape. No doubt when Lallie returned, she would expect to find Hannah gibbering with fright.

She set her lips. Well, she would not give the child that satisfaction. Lallie should see

44

that Miss Smith was not frightened so easily. Hannah vowed that however long the child left her in the Mirror Room, when she eventually returned, she would find Miss Smith just as composed as ever. And with this determination uppermost in her mind, she settled down to wait.

She recited pieces of poetry to herself, went through the multiplication tables, worked out long and complicated arithmetical problems in her head, as the hours passed and she grew more and more hungry, while her throat felt as though it was coated with sand, for the sun on the glass made the room very warm. She drifted off to sleep, and almost fell off the padded seat, then jerked upright. Eventually, she noticed that the room was getting darker, and she seemed to have been sitting there for ever.

A sudden sound roused her. A click and a scrape, and one of the glass panels opened inwards, revealing Mr Armstrong's tall figure, with Lallie and Mrs Jones and Nanny hovering in the background.

'Oh, Miss Smith! So this is where you've been,' Mrs Jones burst out. 'We could not find you anywhere—you've missed luncheon and tea, you poor creature. Miss Lallie thought you might have gone for a walk, and got lost.'

Hannah glanced composedly at Lallie's nervous, defiant face, and managed a cool smile.

'No, I changed my mind and came to have another look at this beautiful room,' she said, fixing her eyes on the child's. 'And when the door shut, I discovered I was unable to get out, so I've been waiting for someone to come. I knew you would find me in the end.' She began to feel her senses swimming in a disconcerting manner. 'I must admit, I should be glad—of something to eat and drink—' she just managed, and Mr Armstrong, who had so far not spoken, came quickly forward to support her. She forgot that she thought him a cold, hard man, and was glad to relax against his strong arm, as he half-lifted, half-assisted her to her feet and towards the door.

'Brandy, Mrs Jones,' he said, in clipped tones. 'And bring something warm for Miss Smith to eat to the drawing-room—and a pot of hot sweet tea.'

'Thank you,' Hannah whispered, her nerves almost at breaking-point now that the ordeal was over, and she deliberately gave Lallie a smile. As she had expected, the girl's face was a study in guilt, then, to Hannah's secret gratification, Lallie burst into tears and ran off down the passage. Hannah felt exhausted, but triumphant. She had obviously passed another test on the prickly road to Lallie's heart.

THREE

Mr Armstrong loomed silently while Hannah recovered herself before the fire in the drawing-room, and drank the hot sweet tea provided by Mrs Jones, and gratefully ate the eggs and toast that were brought to her. When she had finished, she felt distinctly better. It was as she was relaxing over a second cup of tea that her employer spoke.

'I suppose you realize that the whole household has spent almost the entire day searching for you, Miss Smith,' he said coldly. 'You have put us all to a great inconvenience. Even I have had my work interrupted.'

Hannah burned inwardly at the injustice of his words. It was not her fault that she had been locked—deliberately locked—into the Mirror Room.

'I regret the inconvenience, sir,' she answered bitingly, in tones as cold as his own. 'If I had realized that your work was likely to have been disturbed, I might perhaps have been able to break the glass roof of the Mirror Room with a well-aimed shoe, and by sheer force of will managed to levitate myself into the air to the ceiling so that I could have leaned out and acquainted everyone with the fact that I was shut in. As a matter of fact,' she went on, unable to stop the flow of emotion

47

that he had stirred up, 'I did *not* become shut into the room by accident or carelessness. I was locked in by your daughter, who knew perfectly well where I was, but chose to leave me there—in considerable discomfort—until she thought I would have been reduced to a nervous wreck. I can certainly think of more interesting methods of spending my own time than to sit for hours waiting until someone decides to release me from virtual captivity.'

Mr Armstrong frowned.

'Lalage shut you in?' he repeated ominously. 'Then she must be punished. I shall send for her in the morning and reprimand her severely.'

'No, sir,' Hannah pleaded involuntarily. She laid an impulsive hand upon his arm as he sat in the chair beside the settee. 'I—I did not intend to reveal that she was to blame. You see, I believe that she is a child who has—problems. Her mother is dead, and you—'

'Yes, Miss Smith?' he said dangerously.

Hannah gathered her courage together.

'In my opinion, from what I have observed of her behaviour so far, I am coming to the conclusion that she is so wilful and prone to playing tricks such as locking me in the Mirror Room because she lacks—lacks love and affection,' she declared bravely.

Mr Armstrong sprang to his feet, dashing away her arm.

'She has everything a child could need.

48

Clothes—the most expensive I can purchase—whatever she wishes in the way of material things, presents,' he said harshly.

'But you are her father, sir. It is your attention she needs,' Hannah persisted earnestly. 'If you could see your way clear to spending a little more time with her—showing her that you care for her, that you love her—'

Mr Armstrong cut her short.

'When I require your advice, Miss Smith, I shall ask for it,' he interrupted in glacial tones. 'You are impertinent. Good evening.'

And he stalked from the room, outrage in every line of his tall figure. Hannah sank back weakly. What an utterly dreadful day this had been!

*　　　*　　　*

As she lay in bed that night, she found herself going hot with embarrassment at the way she had dared to speak to Mr Armstrong. It was just that she had been so emotionally upset after her ordeal in the Mirror Room, and had let the words slip without thinking. She wondered whether he would dismiss her. The prospect did not dismay her upon her own account, for she was highly qualified, and was not alone in the world—she would probably be able to obtain another post without any trouble, and there was always her family to return to should she decide she had had enough of being independent.

But she had to admit that Mr Armstrong fascinated her in a strange sort of way. She was still not convinced that it had not been he who was responsible for her candles being tampered with, and she found his icy barrier a challenge. She was also becoming increasingly conscious of Lallie's emotional loneliness, and she wished she could bring father and daughter together. But first, she decided, she would have to apologize to Mr Armstrong. He would expect it of her—and perhaps she had outstepped her position as a mere governess in reproving him for not showing more affection for his daughter.

So, after breakfast the next morning—at which Mr Armstrong did not appear, she made her way to the door of his study and knocked resolutely. An impatient; voice said: 'Come in' and she entered the room with her head held high.

Mr Armstrong was sitting at a large desk, surrounded by books and papers. Books lined the walls. He looked up as she walked forward, and enquired:

'Well, what is it?'

'I—I should like to apologize for my hasty words last evening, sir,' Hannah said humbly. 'I fear I was a little overwrought.'

'We will say no more about it, Miss Smith,' he answered, with a dismissive gesture, and Hannah said: 'Thank you, sir.'

50

He bent his dark head to his work again, and as she still lingered, he looked up once more, with an impatient sigh.

'It is Sunday, sir, and I wondered what arrangements are made about attending church,' Hannah explained, apologetically.

He gave her a morose stare from the brown eyes that were so like Lallie's.

'I never attend church, Miss Smith. You may go, if you wish. There is a church in the village—Mrs Jones can inform you of the times of the services—and Mr Jones will get the trap out if you require transport.'

'Oh, that will not be necessary, sir. I can walk,' said Hannah. 'But—Lallie—I mean, Lalage? Does she attend services?'

'Take her if she wishes to go,' he answered offhandedly. 'I personally do not care whether she goes to church or not.'

Hannah was shocked.

'Am I to understand that she has not been brought up to attend church on a Sunday, sir?' she said without thinking, and he stared at her, his dark brows drawn together.

'Do you find that so impossible to believe, Miss Smith?'

'It is certainly an—unusual attitude for a parent to take, not to bring a child up to observe Sunday worship,' Hannah said carefully.

'You are criticizing me again, Miss Smith,' he warned. 'I was brought up as a boy by

51

a father who insisted upon family prayers
morning and evening, and church three
times a day on Sundays.' His lip curled. 'He
was regarded as pious. In fact, he was a man
without feelings, who drove my beloved
mother to an early grave, and made me suffer
humiliation and corporal punishment. I never
knew a loving God—only a cruel and malicious
oppressor. And even when I married, my
happiness was short-lived.' He seemed to be
speaking to himself, his eyes looking back into
the past. 'I thought I had found God through
my wife's simple, sweet beliefs—but within two
years of Lalage's birth, it was discovered that
she was suffering from consumption, and all
my efforts to save her were in vain. Two more
years, and she was dead.' He glanced up at
Hannah, anger in his face. 'So speak to me no
more about church and worship, Miss Smith.'

'I am truly sorry, sir,' Hannah said,
sincerely, 'I—did not realize—'

'I have little enough joy in my life to thank
the Lord for,' he said bitterly.

Hannah did not dare to mention that
perhaps he could find some consolation in his
daughter, for it was obvious that his feelings of
loneliness and deprivation were very deep. She
bobbed a little curtsey, and quietly withdrew.
One part of her was truly sorry for Mr
Armstrong's unhappiness, but her own fighting
spirit cried out that he was allowing himself to
wallow in self-pity, to dwell on past miseries,

and reject the promise of the future. He was a moral coward, she thought, and was glad that her problem lay only with his daughter.

Lallie had been unusually well-behaved in Hannah's presence since the episode of the Mirror Room but, this morning, she had found an old friend and gone out into the yard at the back of the house, where Hannah discovered her with straw in her hair, laughing and giggling as she played at hide-and-seek in the stables with Mair, who was the daughter of one of the women who worked in the kitchen.

'Lallie!' called Hannah, and the girl came running, with Mair, who was taller and a few years older, close behind her.

'Yes, Miss Smith?' Lallie asked. She turned. 'Have you met Mair? She and I made friends the last time I was here—we have a secret pact between us, haven't we, Mair?' And they both collapsed into giggles again.

'Good morning, Mair,' Hannah said, smiling at the girl, though her first impression was that Mair appeared to be sly and furtive-looking, and Hannah did not altogether think she was a fit companion for Lallie, and would lead her into trouble.

'I came to ask whether you wished to attend church,' she told Lallie, who stared at her blankly, then asked in a bored voice:

'Must I?'

'Not if you do not wish to. Your father has said it is for you to decide,' Hannah said, and

53

Lallie put her hands behind her back.

'Do you mind if I don't, Miss Smith? I would really rather stay and play with Mair.'

'Very well then, I will excuse you,' Hannah said. She had expected little else. She turned and went back into the house to freshen herself up and dress for the service. She would just be in good time to walk to the village, she thought, as she pulled on her gloves, and took a last glance in the mirror in her room to make sure her hat was straight and her hair tidy. She picked up her purse and parasol, though the sun was not quite so warm as yesterday, and made her way to the side entrance, which she had discovered by now. Then she set off at a brisk pace for the village.

The square tower of the church was hidden by tall trees, but Hannah knew she would be able to find it without difficulty. As she walked along the narrow lanes, she met up with other people in their Sunday best, who were riding or walking to church or chapel, and the smiles and nods she exchanged with them raised her spirits. In addition, it was delightful to breathe the sweet air, and she was determined to go with Lallie for a nature walk one day soon, where they could gather wild flowers from the hedgerows, and perhaps press them and make a collection. The pale golden sunlight made the lovely scene radiant, and Hannah thought what a pity it was that a man like Mr Armstrong should be unable to find anything

54

in such beauty to stir his senses.

The church proved to be tiny, but obviously extremely old, and Hannah was enchanted with it. She noted, with a quickening of her heart, that Dr Owen Richards was in the congregation, and he smiled warmly when he saw her. Sitting beside him was a lady who reminded Hannah of a porcelain figurine, in her pale blue coat and skirt, with a dainty hat perched on her neatly coiled blonde hair, which was streaked with grey. Obviously this was the doctor's mother, and Hannah noted the deference with which Dr Owen treated her. They must be very close, she thought.

She had forgotten that the service would be in Welsh, but found it fascinating to simply sit and listen to the voice of the preacher, and the voices of the congregation as they sang the hymns. She was astounded by the loveliness of the harmony, and the fact that everyone, without prompting, seemed to sing the appropriate part—soprano, alto, tenor and bass—so that the result was a truly magnificent experience. When the end of the service came, Hannah was sorry, but she felt a calm and peace she had not possessed earlier in the morning descend on her heart.

As she was leaving the church, Dr Owen appeared beside her, and bowed, removing his hat so that the sun gleamed on his fair hair.

'Miss Hannah! We meet again!' he declared, with his rugged grin. 'May I introduce my mother? Mother, this is Miss Hannah Smith, from Bethel House.'

'How do you do, Miss Smith?' said Mrs Richards, holding out a delicate hand, and Hannah took it, returning the smile in the older's woman's grey eyes. 'I wonder how you enjoyed the service? Are you acquainted with the Welsh language?'

'No, but I find it so beautiful, I am content simply to listen. And the singing—I have never heard anything like it,' Hannah replied sincerely.

'Yes, we Welsh pride ourselves on our singing,' Mrs Richards told her, as they sauntered down the village street towards the house that Dr Owen had told her was where he and his mother lived. Mrs Richards stopped at the gate.

'Perhaps, Mother, you would not object if I were to accompany Miss Hannah back to Bethel House?' said Owen, and his mother twinkled at Hannah.

'I need not warn you that my son has an eye for a pretty face. I expect he has already told you of the times he was slapped while away studying,' she said. 'But I hope to see you again, Miss Smith. Perhaps you—and the little girl—would come to tea with me one day?'

'We would be charmed, Mrs Richards,' Hannah replied warmly, and Mrs Richards paused, then went on:

'I would invite Mr Armstrong also, but

I have done so in the past, and he has repeatedly declined my invitations, in the most curt of terms. I fear he is not a very sociable gentleman. He does not mix with anyone here at all when he is in residence at Bethel House.'

'No—he seems very involved with his work,' said Hannah, rather awkwardly, and Mrs Richards smiled.

'But never mind. Would you care to come on Thursday? Would that be convenient?'

'Yes, indeed, and thank you so much for the invitation,' said Hannah, and Mrs Richards gave her a nod, and passed through the garden gate. Owen almost dragged Hannah off down the road.

'Well,' he said without preamble. 'How are you getting on with the unsociable Mr Armstrong and his daughter? Have you settled in here?'

Hannah hesitated, then felt that it would do her good to unburden her mind to the friendly Welshman.

'I must explain first of all that I only joined the household a few days before we came here,' she said, as they walked on through the summer morning, the bees humming in the wild flowers. 'And I am finding things—well, to put it bluntly, a little difficult. You probably know Mr Armstrong and his daughter better than I do. I am only just learning to understand them.'

'And precisely what does that mean?'

questioned Owen, sympathetically.

'Lallie is a most unhappy child,' explained Hannah, frowning. 'She appears to have driven away many governesses before me by—I suspect—playing tricks on them and frightening them. She has already played several on me.' And she recounted the episode of the tapping on the window, and the way Lallie had locked her in the Mirror Room. The young doctor appeared incredulous.

'I would call that extremely unsociable and rude behaviour,' he declared. 'She is quite obviously a badly-brought-up and naughty child.'

'No, I am sure that there is some reason behind what she does,' Hannah replied earnestly. I think it is the lack of her mother, and the fact that her father treats her as though she is nothing but a hindrance to him. He shows no love or affection for her, and he does not seem to care for her mental wellbeing at all. Naturally,' she added in haste. 'I am speaking to you in confidence.'

'I understand. Rest assured that your words shall go no further—not even to my mother,' he said promptly.

'And then Mr Armstrong is such a complex character,' Hannah went on, warming to her theme. 'He has told me a little of his history— apparently he had a rather dreadful father, who destroyed his belief in all things good and beautiful. It was only when he married that he began to feel that there were good things in life. He seems to have adored his young wife.'

'That I can well imagine,' Owen agreed, pulling a stray stem of wild rose from out of her path. 'She was a lovely and adorable creature—sweet, gentle, loving, kind. Her death was a tragedy.'

'Yes, it has made him bitter, and he finds no comfort or consolation in the child,' Hannah told him. 'He is hard and cold, and if he has any happy feelings at all, he seems to have repressed them completely. He is forever working—I don't know what his work is, I presume it is something to do with the estate, but he spends all his time alone in his study.'

'The estate would not take up his every waking moment. It practically runs itself, and he has assistants—manager, and bailiffs,' Owen commented, and Hannah began to wonder just what had been in the books on Mr Armstrong's desk. Now that she came to think of it, they had not been account books, that much she had been able to see even from upside-down. Whatever could he be doing in his study all day? She immediately determined to find out.

'So you are having quite a hard time of it,' Owen said sympathetically, and Hannah added slowly:

'There was something else, too.'

She told him about the candles that had gone out by themselves, and he raised his eyebrows.

'How very odd.'

'Yes, but although Lallie has told me that the house is haunted, I don't believe in ghosts. Some human agency put out those candles by breaking the wicks,' declared Hannah vigorously. 'The only thing is, I am certain that she could not have been responsible, for she was with me all the time, so who else would have wanted to frighten me? I cannot imagine the servants taking it into their heads to do something like that to a mere governess, and I had come to the conclusion that it must have been Mr Armstrong. But—' She shrugged helplessly. 'What could his motive possibly have been? If he does not require my presence, he has only to dismiss me. And, somehow, such subterfuge does not appear to fit in with his character.'

'But nothing else has happened of such a strange nature?' questioned Owen, and Hannah shook her head.

'No. Just that first night, when we arrived—and the Mirror Room.'

'Then perhaps whoever was responsible has stopped their foolish little tricks,' Owen consoled her. 'And as for Lallie, you may well be right when you say she is longing for affection. Children are often naughty in an effort to seek to draw attention to themselves.'

'Yes, I have come across that before,' Hannah nodded.

By this time, they had reached the bridge across the river, and by mutual consent, they came to a standstill, and Hannah rubbed her gloved hand across the stone.

'I wish I could be of some assistance to you,' Owen said, and she smiled warmly.

'Oh, just talking things over with you has been a tremendous help. It has made me see things in perspective. I was becoming too wrapped up in the house and its inhabitants. The incidents I mentioned all seem foolish now, after talking about them and, after all, nothing has occurred to harm me, has it?' Hannah said.

'Well, at least allow me to have the privilege of taking you—and Lallie of course—on a little excursion tomorrow,' offered Owen. He looked up at the sky and added: 'If the weather holds, that is. See, there are clouds coming up. We may have rain before the day is out. But I will take you for a drive tomorrow if you will permit, and show you some of the countryside, including our famous Druidic Circle on top of the hill over there.'

Hannah laughed.

'Nanny has already informed me that the house is inhabited by ghostly Druids,' she told him gaily. 'I should certainly like to see this famous monument for myself.'

'Well, if it is fine, I will call for you and the child at two o'clock,' he declared, and added: 'When you laugh, did you know that you have the most delightful dimple in the corner of your mouth? And I have not told you yet that your hair is like honey, and your eyes a fascinating mixture of blue and green.'

'You should be careful, Dr Owen, I might slap you for being impertinent,' Hannah teased, and they both laughed together. It was at that moment that she looked up and saw the dour figure of Mr Armstrong standing outside the front door, watching her. She sighed.

'There is my employer. I had better go.'

'Until tomorrow, then,' he said, and she agreed readily.

'Until tomorrow.'

She crossed the bridge and went up the short drive. Mr Armstrong called to her.

'Miss Smith!'

'Yes sir?' Hannah answered, and he frowned.

'You seemed to be on very familiar terms with that young man.'

'He is a doctor, sir. I met him when I was out walking, and this morning, he was kind enough to see me home. His mother has invited Lallie and myself to tea on Thursday, and Dr Owen—' She could not help blushing. '– has offered to take us both for a drive tomorrow afternoon, if the weather permits.'

'H'm. So you already have an admirer,' he replied, and Hannah's head went up.

'Dr Owen is not an admirer in the sense you mean sir. I hardly know him. But he is friendly

62

and—very charming. I feel at ease with him.'

'And you do not feel at ease with me?' he demanded bluntly.

Hannah looked down at her purse.

'You are my employer, sir,' she said, at length.

'And can a young lady not feel at ease with her employer?' he demanded again.

'You are—' She looked up. 'You are a very self-contained person, sir. I hardly know what to say.' Then she added honestly: 'If two people are to become—friends, they must meet each other half-way.'

'And you are insinuating that I will not make the effort?' he said drily.

'I did not say that, sir,' Hannah protested, but he had already turned, as though he was bored with the conversation, and disappeared into the house.

Well, let him go, Hannah thought. She had one friend at least in the young doctor.

* * *

When she went to find Lallie, she could not imagine where the girl could be, but eventually discovered her hiding up in the loft amid the straw, and commanded:

'Lallie! Whatever made you climb up there? Come down at once. You might fall.'

A defiant Lallie, accompanied by Mair, descended, and Hannah thought once again that Mair was a bad influence on the child. She would have to speak to Mr Armstrong about it.

'Have you forgotten your position? You are a young lady,' she reprimanded Lallie, as she ushered the girl into the house. 'Look at the state of your clothes. I do believe you follow Mair in every respect, and do anything she tells you.'

'We're blood sisters,' said Lallie, tossing her head. 'We've sworn a blood pact.'

'Blood pact, indeed! What nonsense. Mair is only a servant girl, and you are the young lady of the house. Now come along and get yourself into a fit state for Sunday luncheon. What if your father was to see you like this?' Hannah scolded, and Lallie tossed her head again.

'He wouldn't care.'

'We'll see,' Hannah said ominously, deciding to speak to Mr Armstrong as soon as she could. She really did not like Mair. There was something about the girl that she felt was evil—though she could not have said why. Normally, she would have been pleased that Lallie had a friend in the house—if only it had not been Mair.

*   *   *

She did not like to interrupt Mr Armstrong again that day after his conversation with her on her return from church, and after having intruded into his study once already in the

64

morning, so she did not mention Lallie's behaviour during luncheon, and made sure that the girl spent the afternoon in the house with her sketch-book and pencils. By tea-time, as Dr Owen had forecast, it was raining, and Hannah spent the evening playing cards with Lallie and Nanny. Mr Armstrong was not in evidence. Hannah decided to go to him the next day.

She went to bed with her mind on Lallie and her problems, and fell into a deep sleep, hearing the rain pattering on her windows. By now, she had acquired a lamp, so apart from lighting her way along the corridors, there was no need for her candles. But at some time during the early hours of the morning, she awoke with an uneasy feeling in her mind that all was not well, and lay for a moment, listening.

Then a chill ran up her spine. Lallie had told her that the house was haunted by a drowned baby—and now, in the dark, Hannah could hear it crying, a wailing moan that went on and on in the silence—for the rain had stopped. She sat up. She did not believe in ghosts—and she decided that somebody in the house must be playing a trick on her, and was making the sound of the wailing noise. Yet it seemed so real. Perhaps there *was* a baby in the house, crying alone and unattended.

Hannah was determined that this was one mystery she would not let baffle her, and she

65

climbed out of bed, put on her robe, and, lighting the lamp, lifted it in one hand. Then she opened the door of her room and went out into the dark corridor, with the shadows flickering ahead of her.

FOUR

As noiselessly as she could, Hannah opened the door of Lallie's room, and peeped in, shading the light with her hand. To her surprise, for she had half-expected Lallie to be behind the mysterious noises, she saw that the child was fast asleep, and not feigning, for even as Hannah watched, she turned and murmured in a perfectly natural way, before settling down again beneath her coverlet, her breath coming and going evenly through half-parted lips.

Hannah quietly withdrew into the corridor. She listened, but could still hear the baby's wail, only it seemed to be fainter and more far-off than before. But she was determined to investigate, and she slipped on noiseless feet along the passages, and down the great stairs into the hall. The door to the drawing-room was slightly open, and Hannah could see light inside. Curiosity consumed her, and she pushed open the door, the glow from her own lamp fading before the brighter light of the lamps in the drawing-room.

66

'Ah, Miss Smith,' said a familiar voice, and Hannah blushed, pulling her light robe round her with her free hand. Mr Armstrong was sitting on the settee before the fire, a cigar in one hand, and a glass of wine in the other. He smiled at her confusion. 'To what do I owe the pleasure?' he asked. 'Did you decide to come and keep a lonely man company during a long night's vigil?'

'I am—sorry to disturb you, sir,' Hannah managed to answer, with as much dignity as she could, and she made to withdraw, but he beckoned to her.

'Please, don't go. I am not drunk, Miss Smith, nor have I some secret vice which I am about to reveal to you. The simple fact is that quite often I cannot sleep. And so I sit before the fire, and—brood—think—try to pass the long hours, as best I may.' He turned to look at her fully. 'But you should have been resting long since. It is almost two in the morning. What has disturbed you?'

'I—woke up and heard a noise, sir,' said Hannah, feeling slightly ridiculous. She felt at a distinct disadvantage, in her nightgown and robe, while he was wearing a smoking jacket and trousers. 'It sounded like—like a baby crying. Lallie told me that the house is haunted by the ghost of a drowned baby, who cried, but I do not believe in such things. I felt I must come and investigate, in case there should be a real baby crying.'

To her surprise, his dark face softened.

'You need worry no more, Miss Smith,' he said gently. 'Your tender heart can sleep peacefully. The fact is that a stream runs partly beneath this house, and on days when we have had rain, such as today, it becomes swollen and gurgles along its underground channel making a noise just like the wailing infant. The noise seems to rise through the chimneys so that the sound can only be heard in certain rooms in the house—and the gold room happens to be one of them. On your first night here, when I knocked to make sure you were comfortable, I—well, I had half a mind to warn you, but then I thought it might not rain, or you might not hear the noise, and so I said nothing.'

'I see, sir,' said Hannah. She knew now why Lallie had insisted that she should have that particular room. She could not help the dimple coming to her cheek. *What* a little schemer Lallie was! No wonder her other governesses had been unable to cope with her.

'Will you sit down for a moment, Miss Smith?' Mr Armstrong asked in an unusually gentle tone. 'Or am I keeping you from your beauty sleep?'

'Not at all, sir. I am wide awake, and do not think I should be able to fall asleep for quite some time, after this,' said Hannah truthfully.

'You will perhaps take a little wine? That will help you to sleep again,' Mr Armstrong suggested, and poured her a glass, coming over with it to where she had sat down in the big chair at the side of the fire. She had extinguished her lamp, and set it down for the time being on the sideboard, amid the china ornaments.

'Tell me about yourself, while you drink your wine, Miss Smith,' said Mr Armstrong, gruffly. 'I know you are a courageous young lady, that you are extremely attractive, that you do not shirk unpleasant tasks. Are you alone in the world?'

'No sir, I have my parents and a sister who is married. They live in London,' said Hannah, and he raised his brows.

'Then why do you choose to work as a governess? Is your family in impoverished circumstances? Do they need the money?'

'Oh, far from it, sir. I could live a life of leisure if I chose, but I wanted to be useful in the world, to see something of life. I suppose I am just independent by nature,' Hannah answered. 'And I love children—most children,' she added, thinking of Mair.

'I hope you are not referring to Lalage,' he said, and she turned to him impulsively.

'Oh, no, sir. I think I am beginning to understand your daughter and—hopefully— to gain her trust a little. I was thinking of the friend she has here—a girl called Mair. I believe she is the daughter of one of the women who works in the kitchen. I believe she is a bad influence on Lallie—I mean, Lalage.

69

She strikes me as an—an evil child.'

'Evil?' he questioned. 'In what way?'

Hannah shrugged helplessly.

'I don't know, sir. But some children seem to have a sort of evil aura about them—a maliciousness. And Lallie spoke of a blood pact they had made—I don't like Mair,' she admitted frankly.

'I cannot say I know of the child in question,' Mr Armstrong said, frowning into the fire. 'But I will ask Mrs Jones about her tomorrow. She will no doubt be taken by surprise at my actually appearing to be interested in the goings-on in the kitchen,' he went on, and smiled briefly. 'As you know, Miss Smith, I take no interest in very much around me so long as my employees carry out their work in a satisfactory manner. She will think I am a changed man. As perhaps I am,' he said, in a low voice.

Hannah made no comment on this point. She was quite enjoying herself sitting in the warmth of the fire, with the good wine flowing through her body. And Mr Armstrong seemed to be in a mellow mood. She found him remarkably good company when he was not being disagreeable, and it emboldened her to ask hesitantly:

'You often speak of your work, sir. Might I enquire are you engaged on any specific piece of work? Or simply on household business?'

'I talk of my work to no-one,' he replied

70

coldly, and made a gesture with his hand. 'You would not understand.'

'I—I am sorry, sir. I did not mean to pry,' Hannah answered hastily, thinking she had been wrong in deciding he was in a mellow mood.

'If you must know, I am engaged in translating some of the work of Aeschylus into English. There,' he said, and was obviously disconcerted when her face lit up.

'Not the *Oresteia?*' she breathed excitedly, and he asked sharply:

'And what do you know about the Oresteia, Miss Smith?'

'Oh, sir, I think the trilogy is a most marvellous work. I especially admire *Agamemnon*. The story of Clytemnestra has always fascinated me,' Hannah told him, and he gazed at her for a long time in the leaping flames of the fire and the soft glow of the lamps.

'Well, well, Miss Smith. May I take it you have read the works in question?' he demanded, and she nodded.

'Over and over, sir. I wish I could visit Greece to see the places where these wonderful legends and heroic tales took place. Italy, too.' She smiled. 'Now I understand why you have named your daughter Lalage—the poet Horace—'

'Do you mean to tell me,' demanded Mr Armstrong incredulously, 'that you are familiar

71

with Greek and Roman literature? Surely not in the original?'

'But of course, sir,' said Hannah, and added with an impish smile: 'I could quote you some, to prove my claim, if you wish.' Her face took on a soft glow. 'Imagine! In the letters of Pliny, he actually described the eruption of Vesuvius and the destruction of Pompeii. He was an eye-witness to that very sight! And we can read his words as if we were there ourselves, all those years ago. When I first read his account of the tragedy, my whole frame was seized with a chill of excitement and incredulity. To have actually seen the volcano erupt—to have been there—'

Mr Armstrong poured himself another glass of wine, and his movement roused Hannah from her reverie.

'Forgive me, sir,' she said primly. 'I fear I was—rather carried away.'

'Not at all, Miss Smith. That is how I too feel when I read the work of the ancient Greeks and Romans. That is why I lose myself in the powerful tragedies of the *Oresteia*—it is my escape from the mundane life I must live today. They thought on such a grand scale,' Mr Armstrong said, and his dark eyes were full of excitement, 'which communicated the whole problem of fate and destiny—our place in the world—'

'Everything is ordained—the patterns of life work themselves out,' Hannah agreed,

72

eagerly. 'Oh, sir, I wonder—would it be too presumptuous of me to ask to see your work? I would so much like to read your English translation of the work of Aeschylus.'

'I have let no-one read it—I have finished the *Agememnon* and am at present working on the second part, the *Libation-Bearers,*' Mr Armstrong told her, his eyes smiling into hers. 'But—I think I shall let you read *Agememnon,* Miss Smith, I would value your opinion.'

'An English translation. Perhaps you will publish it, sir,' Hannah suggested enthusiastically. 'Then you will be famous.'

Somehow, without quite knowing how, she found they were sitting close together on the settee, and their talk on Greek and Roman literature had brought them near to each other. She was suddenly conscious of the touch of his shoulder against her own, the fact that he was holding one of her hands, and the nearness of his dark head. She blushed furiously, and the realization of their position seemed to strike him at the same time, for he tilted up her chin so that she was forced to look into his brown eyes.

'Do you know how long it has been since I have kissed a woman, Miss Smith?' he asked, very softly, and Hannah's lips parted. She felt as though she might faint. Strange sensations were making her body feel weak. Somehow, the firelight and the wine she had drunk made her conscious that whatever he might choose

73

to do, she would not reject him.

'No, sir,' she whispered, and he touched her unbound hair.

'Your hair is yellow silk,' he murmured, and picked up a long strand, and lifted it to his lips. 'You are not real, are you, Miss Smith? I am sitting here before the fire, and I have fallen asleep. You are something that has come to me in a dream. The Miss Smith I know would never sit here in my arms with her unbound hair like a shower of gold in the firelight, and never raise her lips to mine—as you are doing. But since I am dreaming, and this is only a dream-kiss, then I will kiss you.'

Hannah closed her eyes as his lips came down on hers, at first softly and tenderly, then with a passion that roused her to respond. She could feel the hardness of his chest against her breasts, and his hands on each side of her face, twining themselves in her hair. If this was a dream, she thought, slightly dazed by wine, then it was a dream from which she did not want to wake. Tentatively, she lifted a hand, and caressed his thick dark hair, and for what seemed an eternity, time seemed to stand still, so that she was only conscious of his warm, urgent lips, and his body close beside her.

Then he released her, and rose from the settee, going to stand at the other end of the room, his back to her.

'Forgive me, Miss Smith,' he said in a hard, cold tone. 'Perhaps you had better return to your room.'

Hannah pushed back her dishevelled hair, pulled her robe about her, and rose also. For some reason, she felt absurdly disappointed, and wanted to burst into tears. She lit her lamp, picked it up, and prepared to leave the room. Still he had not looked at her but, as she opened the door, he said:

'I would be grateful if you could forget that this—this episode ever happened. Goodnight, Miss Smith.'

'Goodnight, sir,' she answered, and pulled the door closed behind her, leaning against it with an odd knot of desolation in her heart. Then she made her way along the corridors and mechanically got back into her own bed. In a few moments, she was asleep.

*   *   *

When she awoke in the morning, Hannah's first feeling was one of utter shame. Had she really sat before the fire with Mr Armstrong, locked in a close embrace? She could not imagine how she would ever face him at breakfast, and she tried to cool her burning cheeks with cold water. She dressed in a particularly severe suit, and coiled her hair tightly back from her face. He would think her a woman of no principles at all, a thorough wanton. Still, she had to face him, and she decided to get it over with as quickly as

75

possible.

But as she entered the dining-room, where Lallie was already eating her breakfast, and Mr Armstrong was helping himself from the hot-plates, he turned and greeted her in his usual absent manner.

'Good morning, Miss Smith.'

'Good morning, sir,' she answered, and went to get her own breakfast with her head held high. But he behaved in such an ordinary way that she began to wonder whether she had in fact dreamed the whole thing. Perhaps that was the answer—she had imagined it—the noise of the crying baby, the discussion on Greek and Roman literature, that beautiful, beautiful embrace. The thought gave her confidence. Of course—it had all been a dream. She would never have behaved so irresponsibly—and she could not for a moment imagine him saying the lovely words that the man in her dream had uttered nor being tender and loving. When Mr Armstrong embraced someone, it would be in a cold, calculating fashion. Hannah sat down with a distinct sense of relief.

The rain had cleared, and the day was slightly misty, promising to be sunny and warm.

'What are you planning to do with yourself this morning, Lallie?' asked Hannah, and Lallie gave her a distinctly mulish look.

'I don't know,' she said.

'Well, I suggest that we visit the village, and you can do some sketches of the old church. It's quite beautiful, with carvings and old archways,' said Hannah. 'Or you could sketch some of the wild flowers, Lallie. I thought we might go for a nature walk, and take some books I have, to identify the different plants and shrubs of the hedgerows. We could even start a collection of pressed plants, and label them. Then you'd have something to remember the country by when we go back to London.'

Lallie pushed a piece of bacon round on her plate.

'Mair will be waiting for me,' she muttered.

'I've told you before, I don't approve of your seeing Mair,' Hannah answered sharply. 'She is just a village girl, and you are a young lady.' She recalled that she had mentioned Mair in her dream, but concluded that it was simply that the girl was playing on her mind, for Mr Armstrong showed no sign that he had heard anything about Mair before.

Hannah turned to him.

'Lalage appears to have made a friend of one of the children of the workers in the kitchen, sir,' she said, and he raised his brows, as though in surprise. 'I must confess, I am not happy about the association. The girl—Mair—leads Lallie into dangerous and—in my opinion—unsuitable situations, and I would be happy if they could be parted.'

77

Lallie startled both of them by springing to her feet, two spots of angry colour in her cheeks.

'Mair is the only friend I've got,' she cried, half in tears. 'She's the only person I can play with. I don't want to be parted from her. It's—it's not fair!'

Hannah turned to Mr Armstrong in horror. She herself thought it a good sign that Lallie felt able to let her real feelings out, but how would he take it? To her amazement, he was showing no sign of the cold fury she had expected, but was thoughtfully drinking his tea. Carefully, he replaced the cup, then said:

'How would it be if I were to take a little time off from my work to accompany you? And Miss Smith, of course.'

Lallie looked as though she could not believe her ears, but her delight was obvious.

'Would you, Papa? Would you really come for a walk with me?'

'We are here on holiday, Lalage,' he told her calmly. 'Perhaps we should spend more of our time together.' He gave Hannah a dry look, and added: 'Why, Miss Smith took me to task in quite a fearsome fashion only the other day for neglecting you.'

'Oh, sir—' Hannah protested, her face bright red, but he waved her words aside.

'I have considered what she said, and I believe she is right.' He glanced at Lallie. 'Well? Would a nature walk with Miss Smith and your crusty old father be more amusing than playing with your friend Mair, do you think?'

'Oh, *yes,* Papa!' Lallie cried gleefully and, for a moment, Hannah thought the child was about to throw her arms round his neck. Then she recollected herself, and said primly: 'I'll go and get ready, and collect my sketch-book.'

As she rushed from the room, Mr Armstrong raised his brows at Hannah.

'So. Does that satisfy you, Miss Smith? I cannot promise for how long I will be able to continue to behave in the manner of an exemplary father, but I did consider your words, and you are quite correct. I saw from Lalage's reaction how much she required my attention.'

'It will mean the world of difference to her, sir,' Hannah said impulsively. 'If you begin to take an interest in her doings, and especially her achievements.' She paused, then went on: 'I can set you a task, sir. Lallie will show no-one her sketches and drawings. If you could persuade her to show you, by displaying a genuine interest in her work, then I think a great bridge between you will have been built. I have not abused her confidence by looking in her sketch-book, but I should not be at all surprised to find she has real talent, and if this is the case, then we should encourage it. Extra drawing lessons, for instance, with a proper art master—'

'Why, what a domineering person you are. Miss Smith,' Mr Armstrong declared, finishing his tea. 'I do believe you will be taking over my work in running the household next. Don't you ever unbend a little, or are you always the true emancipated female, fighting for her rights?'

Hannah recalled her dream, and her cheeks slowly went scarlet, but when she looked at him, there was no indication in his face that he had meant anything other than what he had said. Reassured that it had all been a dream indeed, she was able to answer in a spirited manner:

'I was born beneath the sign of Aries, sir, and Arians, according to what I have read, are always domineering. So you see, I cannot help my nature.'

'Well, all I can say is that you must have been more than a match for any governess *you* may have had,' he declared, and the flicker of a smile crossed his face.

Mr Armstrong was obviously making a heroic effort to change his ways, and the nature walk was a great success. In the bright sunshine, the little party sauntered along the lanes to the village, where Hannah said:

'Now you can show me around, Lallie. You must know Bethel well, as you have been here before.'

'Papa knows it better than me,' said Lallie, proudly. 'Did you come here a lot when you were wooing Mama?' she asked her father, and a shadow passed across his face.

'That was a long time ago, Lalage. But I can tell you something about the church. It is named for a saint—a Welsh one, I believe. It is very old. There is a particularly interesting carving over here—' and he led the way through the churchyard to a corner where he pointed to one of the weathered stones a little above Hannah's head. 'That is supposed to be the saint's face. Do you think you could draw it?'

'I'll draw it especially for you,' declared Lallie, and settled down on a tombstone, her head bent over her sketch-pad, while Hannah and Mr Armstrong wandered through the graves, commenting idly on the inscriptions, which of course were in Welsh.

'Don't you find this a beautiful place, sir?' asked Hannah. 'The quiet little village—your lovely house, and the river running by it—the mountains and the hills?'

He looked round.

'I am not used to noticing nature, Miss Smith. You will have to open my eyes,' he declared, and asked: 'What do you see?'

'That the sky is blue, with little fleecy white clouds, and the trees surrounding this ancient old building are a delicate shade of green, sir,' Hannah answered obediently.

'The world has lost its colour for me, Miss Smith,' he said regretfully. 'I see—how does the Bible put it?—through a glass, darkly. One cannot change overnight, and I have spent the years since my wife died as a recluse. I see the sky, and the trees, and they do not move me.'

'But you cannot mourn forever, sir,' Hannah said impulsively. 'Why, this morning, you have taken a great step. Lallie is thrilled at your attention. Do you not feel some corresponding warmth towards her? Do you not gain pleasure from the pleasure you have given her by your company? She has hung upon your every word, every gesture. She would like to hold your hand, to run races with you in the grass, to throw her arms about you—but she can hardly believe you are the same father she has always known. She is afraid of being rejected.'

He gave a short laugh.

'At least, then, I shall have some respite. I am afraid I could not respond to her in that way. I *should* reject her. Miss Smith, you have opened my eyes to one thing at least. I do not know my own daughter.'

'Then try to get to know her—slowly, sir. Let things happen as they will,' urged Hannah, earnestly. 'Lallie will perhaps be the one to open your eyes for you, for you to see the blue of the sky and the green of the trees again.'

'I will do what I can—I promise you no more,' he said harshly, and she coloured.

'I apologize, sir. I was being unduly familiar.'

A constraint seemed to have settled between them, and they walked on in silence, until Lallie came running, her drawing in her hand.

'Here, Papa, it is finished. Do you like it? I took especial care, since it was for you.'

Mr Armstrong studied the lines of the pencil drawing.

'Why, Lalage—' he exclaimed, and stopped. When he continued, there was a note of interest in his voice. 'I believe Miss Smith is right—you have a distinct talent for drawing. When we return to London, you shall have drawing lessons with a really good art master.'

'Oh, Papa, could I?' cried Lallie, her face alight.

'And I am sure your Papa is so proud of this drawing you did especially for him that he will pin it up in the wall of his study,' prompted Hannah, hoping Mr Armstrong would follow her lead. To her relief, he did.

'Certainly, I shall do it as soon as we get back home,' he said, and Hannah was convinced he could not possibly remain unaffected by the glowing delight and pride that shone from Lallie's brown eyes.

On the way home, she hopped and skipped ahead of them, picking flowers from the hedgerows and bringing them for Hannah to identify.

'I don't know much, but we'll have a look in my book once we get back,' Hannah promised, and Lallie said eagerly:

'And could we press them and keep them,

83

Miss Smith, the way you suggested? I thought of calling it 'My Country Note-book'.'

'That's a splendid idea,' Hannah approved, and when they returned to the house, and went to their rooms to prepare for luncheon, she felt a glow of virtue. Not only had Mr Armstrong drawn Lallie's attention away from Mair, but he had actually begun to come out of his shell. She hoped he would continue to spare some of his attention for his daughter, and not retreat back into the dark recesses of his previous hermit-like existence.

It was with a light heart that she went down the stairs to the dining-room. This afternoon Dr Owen was coming to take them for a drive and, tonight, she and Lallie would press the flowers, and begin work on Lallie's country scrap-book. The day was going far better than she could ever have dreamed.

FIVE

Hannah had sensibly decided that in her position as a governess, she would look outlandish in gowns frothing with frills of chiffon and lace, so her wardrobe consisted largely of sensible—but well-cut—dark skirts and blouses which, however, were made of silk and were heavily-trimmed with Chantilly lace. The high necks with their stiff, wired collars

84

showed off her own long slender neck, and her belts emphasized her slim waist.

She had, however, brought several gowns with her, and she debated whether to wear one for the drive with Dr Owen, but in the end decided to keep to her 'uniform' of crisp white blouse and black skirt, her hair piled up with her boater finishing off the picture.

She knew that the black and white became her fair colouring, and as the trap turned into the drive and she and Lallie went forward to meet him, she was aware of the admiration in his eyes.

After her morning with her father, Lallie was in a very good humour, and quite prepared to enjoy a drive to see the Druidic Circle. It was a pity, however, that Nanny, on hearing that she would not be required to walk, had decided to accompany them, and was also waiting in her long black coat, a rusty black hat set firmly upon her head.

'Good afternoon, Dr Owen. You will not mind if Nanny accompanies us, will you?' called Hannah, as Lallie began to scramble into the trap, and he smiled.

'The more the merrier. Good afternoon, Lallie. I don't believe we've ever been properly introduced. Will it suffice as an introduction if I tell you that I have brought a large picnic basket with me?'

'A picnic basket? Oh—*yes!*' cried Lallie eagerly. 'Come along Miss Smith. Come on,

Nanny, don't dither. We're going on a picnic!'

'Quite a charming picture,' drawled a familiar voice, and Hannah turned as she took her place in the trap, her colour mounting. Mr Armstrong was standing by the open front door, his arms folded, his attitude quite different from that of the morning. His thick dark brows were drawn grimly together.

'Oh, sir, may I present Dr Owen Richards? My employer, Mr Armstrong,' she said, and Dr Owen spoke impulsively.

'Good afternoon, sir. I'm delighted to be able to meet you at last. My mother has invited you to take tea with us on several occasions before—perhaps, since your daughter and Miss Smith are coming on Thursday, you would care to accompany them this time.'

'I think not,' said Mr Armstrong, in clipped tones. 'But thank you for the invitation, doctor. I do not make social calls.'

Then, deliberately, he turned his back on the little group, and was lost in the dimness of the hall. Something of his gloom lingered, and Hannah spoke brightly to try and dispel it.

'Now, are we all ready? We're settled, doctor. Drive on to the Wonders of Wales.'

'The Druidic Circle isn't really a Wonder of Wales, you know, Miss Smith,' Lallie said in a superior tone. 'But there are seven wonders. There's a rhyme about them—only I can't quite remember all of it. I'll try and remember, and write it out for you tonight, after we've pressed the flowers.'

'Thank you, dear,' said Hannah, holding onto her hat as the trap swung out of the drive and along the lane, the dainty little mare picking up her feet, and the fragrance of the wild flowers wafting on the gentle sunny breeze.

'This is heaven,' said Hannah happily.

'Not quite. But something very close to it, don't you think?' Dr Owen replied, pleased at her enjoyment.

*   *   *

It would have been a wonderful outing except for the inhibiting presence of Nanny. Hannah had by now discovered that Nanny thought about her own creature comforts first, and her next preoccupation was in letting Lallie behave in as outrageous a manner as she chose. She encouraged what she called 'spirit'—which meant that when Lallie clambered precariously onto one of the large stones that made up the Druidic Circle, and announced loudly that she was going to jump, Nanny urged comfortably: 'That's it, my dearie.'

Hannah had paled.

'Lallie, that stone is far too high. Climb down carefully *at once,* do you hear?' she snapped, her anxiety making her voice sharper than she had intended.

Lallie looked defiant.

'I'm jumping,' she said, and Dr Owen leaped forward to catch her. She landed unsteadily in his arms, and Hannah leaned over her.

'You silly girl! You might have broken a leg.'

'Oh, leave her be. I like to see a child with spirit,' said Nanny, and Hannah turned, wishing she could tell Nanny something very unladylike about her indulging the child. Nanny looked back at her, and there was something in her gaze that disturbed Hannah. Perhaps she had been wrong in thinking that Nanny had accepted her. It was almost as though the old woman took a delight in encouraging Lallie to defy her governess. For a moment, Hannah's thoughts strayed to the candles that had gone out by themselves. Perhaps it was Nanny who wanted to get rid of her—or maybe Nanny had cooked up some plan with Lallie herself so that they took it in turns to frighten Hannah.

Owen soon smoothed the atmosphere over, however, with his cheerful bantering and the production of the picnic basket, and as they sat on the smaller stones (the grass was wet after yesterday's rain, Hannah insisted) eating the sandwiches and homemade cakes and pies that Mrs Richards had provided, he entertained Lallie with tales of his life as a doctor.

'Did you ever see a body?' Lallie demanded ghoulishly, and he considered her question carefully.

'Well, a doctor does see people die, you know. Sometimes, if he can't cure them.'

'No, I mean a *real* body,' Lallie insisted, and Owen leaned forward with a conspiratorial air.

'When you come to tea on Thursday, I will let you see something better than a body. In the cupboard at home, I have a skeleton! There!'

'A real one?' Lallie was awed.

Owen leaned back.

'Ah, that would be telling, wouldn't it? But I'll let you see him—I call him Henry—and you can judge for yourself.'

'Doesn't he frighten you?' asked Lallie, after a moment, and Owen laughed.

'Old Henry? No, he's one of the family now. I used to use him when I was studying anatomy in Medical School.'

Lallie regarded him solemnly, then she asked, with an unexpected change of tone:

'Are you Miss Smith's friend?'

'Well—I hope so,' Owen answered, with an ardent glance in Hannah's direction. Hannah knew that he was disappointed because they had no chance to talk alone.

'Will you be my friend too?' asked Lallie, and the rugged young Welshman's face softened.

'Certainly, Miss Lalage. We'll swear a friendship pact. Here—shake hands on it. We vow to be friends for ever and ever.'

Importantly, Lallie placed her hand in his,

89

then he said: 'And now we have to turn round and spit on the ground.'

Nanny cackled unexpectedly.

'The old stones still see magic rites being performed,' she said dreamily.

Lallie was enchanted, however, especially at being told to spit. To her, that was so unladylike it *must* be important, and Hannah smiled inwardly. What a way Owen had with children. And what a good day it had been for Lallie. First her father's attention, and now a new friend in Owen.

She sat while Owen and Lallie—now sworn friends for ever—shared the same stone to eat their sandwiches, and let her gaze wander from the top of the hill where the circle of stones stood, some half-buried in the earth, to the green prospect around her, with the silver thread of the river running through it, and the afternoon sunlight coating the scene with gold. Far away, she could see the tops of what she thought might be Snowdonia, with their high rocky crags wreathed in mist or cloud—or just her imagination. Wales was a land where one's imagination could run riot. And the peace and tranquility of the scene sank deeply into her heart and mind. She would not object to living here forever, she thought.

*   *   *

But when they returned home, reality was

waiting for her in the dark figure of Mr Armstrong, who said, after Owen had driven off with the promise to see Lallie and herself on Thursday at his mother's home for tea: 'Would you come into my study for a moment, Miss Smith?'

He seemed to have forgotten his good intentions towards his daughter and his tentative friendliness towards herself. He was as grim as on the day she had first seen him and, as she stood in his study, he paced the carpet in just the way he had paced the library in the house in Belgravia.

'I have made enquiries in the kitchen,' he said abruptly. 'You mentioned the child—what was her name?—Mair. She is the daughter of one of the maids who helps out here. You can tell her that she is not to associate with Lalage in the future—threaten her with whatever punishment you wish. This is a domestic matter, so I will leave it in your hands.' His eyebrow lifted sardonically. 'Your very capable hands, Miss Smith.'

So he had not forgotten. Hannah spoke warmly. 'Thank you, sir,' she said. 'I think that if you are able to spend a little more time with Lallie—I mean, Lalage—and pay more attention to her—'

'I have told you that I will try. I can promise no more than that. My mood is not always—equable,' interrupted Mr Armstrong sharply. 'Thank you, Miss Smith. Good afternoon.'

He lowered his head to the papers on his desk, and Hannah coloured.

'Good afternoon, sir,' she replied, and quietly left the study. She went immediately in search of Mair, and found her, as she had expected, in the stables. To her relief, Lallie was not there.

'Mair, I must tell you that from now on, you are not to speak to Miss Lalage or play with her. You are not a young lady of her station, and she must be brought up to know her place in society,' she told the girl, not unkindly.

There was a silence, then Mair said expressionlessly: 'Yes, miss.'

'You do understand, don't you, Mair? If I hear of you trying to pass messages to Lallie or involving her in secret games, I will have to tell her father, and you will not be allowed to remain at this house any longer,' Hannah went on, feeling it expedient to add: 'And neither will your mother'—a threat she had no intention of keeping. But Mair must be warned off.

The girl looked at her, then her eyes slid away.

'I understand, miss,' she said in the same expressionless tone.

'Good,' said Hannah and, with a nod, she left the stables and went out into the late afternoon sunlight, feeling that a difficult task had been satisfactorily accomplished.

Lallie was absorbed in the wild flowers that they had picked that morning, and Hannah fetched her book of wayside plants for them to identify and press the dainty blossoms and grasses and leaves. Almost before they knew it, the time had come to dress for dinner.

Since they were officially on holiday, Hannah did not always feel it necessary to change her gown, but tonight, after Mr Armstrong's brusqueness in the afternoon, she wanted to gain his attention again and try and lull him into the friendly, confidential mood of the morning. She told herself it was for Lallie's sake, so that he would pay more attention to his daughter, and perhaps even sit with them after dinner, but she had to be honest with herself and admit that she wanted some of his attention for herself too. She wanted to know why he was so unpredictable, why he was so sullen at one moment and so approachable the next. She found him a challenge.

So when they went to their rooms to wash and freshen up in the hot water that the maids had carried from the kitchen, Hannah looked through her wardrobe and decided to wear a new gown, which was of eau-de-nil chiffon, with touches of slightly darker green, and a green lace collar that framed her shoulders.

She was sitting before her mirror in the soft twilight, dreamily brushing her hair before donning the gown, and debating whether she needed to light a candle or a lamp, but reluctant to disturb the softness of the approaching night, when she was suddenly aware that not only her own face was reflected in the mirror, but that there was movement in the darker depths of the glass, which reflected the window behind her, its curtains drawn back.

A cold chill ran up Hannah's spine and her hand, holding her brush, was frozen with horror. She could see her own face, startled and with wide glittering eyes, but deeper in the recesses of the glass something was lurking—another face, a white, anonymous face with black gashes where the eyes should have been, and a cloud of corn-blonde hair drifting as thought the dead face in the window was drowned and the currents of water were moving the hair.

Hannah had seen the portrait of Caroline Armstrong that hung above the fireplace in the drawing-room, and recognized the heart-shaped features and the soft corn-coloured hair—though it had been tied back in the portrait with a ribbon, and she had been holding a wide-brimmed straw hat—she had posed dressed as a shepherdess. For one horrified moment, her heart almost stopped, and she whispered involuntarily: 'Caroline!'

The face moved gently, and at the same time, Hannah's commonsense returned. This

94

was another attempt to try and frighten her. She shut her eyes for a second, took a deep breath, and then turned slowly—though it took all her reserves of courage—and faced the thing in the window. Then she swallowed hard. It had gone. The curtain drapes framed only the soft sapphire and silver of a summer evening, with the hills dark as crouching animals in the distance.

In a moment, Hannah was across the room, the window wide, forgetting her state of undress. She looked up and down the walls for any sign of the vision, but there was nothing to show where it had come from. Shaking slightly, both with her recent panic, and with mounting anger, she threw on her green chiffon robe and ran through into Lallie's room.

It was obviously not Lallie who had been the culprit this time, for she was engaged in buttoning the hooks down the back of her white dress, her face scarlet with difficulty, and had obviously been doing this for the last few minutes.

'Can you manage, dear?' asked Hannah, arrested in her impulse to dash into Nanny's room and see what Nanny was doing.

'Not—really. I hate hooks,' panted Lallie, and Hannah quickly performed the rest of the task, said: 'I'll be back in a second,' and ran along the corridor to Nanny's room. It would be just like the old woman, she thought, to imagine that a vision of Caroline would frighten her, and she knocked briskly, and, hardly waiting for Nanny's slow 'Come in', opened the door.

Nanny was in her usual black, putting the finishing touches to her hair, which would never stay quite in its coil on the top of her head. She turned, startled.

'Miss Smith! You're not even dressed! You'll be late for dinner.'

'Have you—did you—?' Hannah burst out impulsively, then checked herself, for what could she say? 'Was it you who just hung a model of a face resembling Caroline's outside my window, Nanny?' Quite obviously Nanny had not—or if she had, her methods were such that Hannah would never detect them by direct means.

And that left only one person, she thought bitterly, as she asked Nanny for an unnecessary hair-pin she did not need, and went slowly back to her own room, pausing to look in at Lallie on the way, to straighten her sash and tell her she looked very nice.

'Now, give your hair a good brushing, dear, and I'll be back in a minute or two to tie your ribbon,' she told the child.

She pulled the curtains in her own room, hurried into her eau-de-nil gown, which fortunately was not a difficult dress to fasten. It hung in soft folds over her rustling petticoat—although Hannah had heard that rustling petticoats were becoming out-of-
96

fashion amongst the leaders of society. So too were trained skirts, although her gown had only the smallest of trains at the back. Quickly she adjusted her collar, and coiled her hair into a knot low on her neck instead of piling it in its usual bouffant style that took a lot longer to get ready.

When she was satisfied, she took a last glance in the long mirror, decided that her cheeks were too flushed from her recent experience, and brushed a little rice powder over them. More and more women were enamelling their faces as actresses did, but Hannah rarely used her rice powder or coloured her lips, having no need to. But she could not go down to dinner looking dishevelled. Sensible—sane—capable—that was what Mr Armstrong had called her—and she must look the part.

Thinking of Mr Armstrong brought her back to the fact that he was the only person who might have perpetrated the trick of hanging a modelled face outside her window. Lallie and Nanny had not done it—Hannah was certain of that—and as she assisted Lallie with her hair ribbon and accompanied the child down the stairs to dinner, her thoughts were deep and purposeful.

The model would have had to have been let out of the window one storey above Hannah's own, and then quickly drawn back up and the window shut. For of course, she did not believe for a moment that she had really seen Caroline's ghostly face. No, it was definitely another attempt to frighten her into leaving.

During the soup, she managed to enquire carelessly who slept above her in the higher corner room, saying that their view would probably be just as lovely—if not lovelier—than her own.

'Oh, that's one of the guest bedrooms that's always kept covered with dust-sheets, unless there's a big house-party. There's never been one, not that I can remember,' Lallie told her, a little wistfully. 'But you're right, Miss Smith, the view is nice. After all, there's only the attics and then you're on the roof if you go any higher up.' Her face became animated. 'Would you like to go on the roof? I can show you how to get there?'

Hannah shuddered slightly. 'No thank you, Lallie dear. I'm afraid I am one of those people who would suffer an attack of vertigo if I were to find myself up on top of somewhere as high as this house.' She paused, then went on carelessly: 'I suppose the rooms that are kept shut up are not locked?'

'Locked? No, why should they be? Sometimes the maids go in to clean up a bit. Usually when we are here, and the extra staff is available they give the house a bit of a going-over. Why?' asked Lallie curiously.

Hannah shrugged.

'I just thought I might like to go up and

98

see the view from the upper window some day,' she said, deliberately carelessly. 'I was wondering whether the church and village would be visible from a little higher up than my own window.' She changed the subject, speaking brightly. 'Well, Lallie dear, you have had quite an adventurous day, haven't you? I expect you are tired.'

'Oh, not too tired to do a little more of my flowers before bed-time,' protested Lallie vehemently. 'If we don't do them quickly, they'll die, Miss Smith.' She turned to her father, who was eating in dour silence. 'Papa, would you like to see how far we have progressed? Or—or even help us?' Mr Armstrong looked up. His face was shuttered and dark.

'I—think not. Not tonight, Lalage,' he said, and Hannah, at the disappointment that flashed across Lallie's features, said:

'Well, I have an idea. Tomorrow, we'll set up the croquet hoops on the lawn—I saw a croquet set somewhere among the things in the yard, and I expect Mr Jones will be able to find mallets and a ball for us. And perhaps your Papa would feel like taking some exercise if you were to ask him, Lallie dear.' She leaned across and whispered loudly: 'Why don't you invite him to a game of croquet?'

Across the table, her eyes pleaded with Mr Armstrong, and when Lallie enquired importantly: 'Papa, would you care for a game

99

of croquet tomorrow—should the weather permit, of course?' he managed a half-smile.

'I dare say I could find the time for one game—or even two,' he told his daughter, and she squealed with delight.

'I'll beat you, Papa, see if I don't!' she cried, her mercurial spirits soaring again. Hannah gave Mr Armstrong her warmest smile, but he did not smile back. Instead, he gave her a long, enigmatic stare, before returning his attention to the roast lamb that had just been placed before him.

Hannah's thoughts went back to their original course. She was sure that Mr Armstrong did not object to her efforts to further his relationship with his daughter, but he appeared at times to have a grudge against her personally, simply because she was herself. His moods fluctuated so unpredictably. Sometimes he seemed to go out of his way to be friendly towards her, and at other times— like now, for instance—he would stare at her with his brows drawn together and an expression almost of hate.

Hannah began to wonder what his thoughts towards herself really were. He had mourned his wife for ten years—he did not appear to have any interest in other women. And then she could not forget the candles that had gone out by themselves, and the face she had just seen at the window—Caroline's face.

Had his wife's death twisted his mind?

Was he haunted by the image of his sweet, lovely bride who had died so tragically, that he had strange dark moods where he did not, perhaps, even know what he was doing? Did he really want her in the house—or would he feel relieved if she left? She even found herself wondering whether her employer was—just a little—mad. It was a frightening thought.

*   *   *

After dinner, the ladies retired to the drawing-room, leaving Mr Armstrong to his port and a cigar. Nanny, declaring she had walked far too much that day—although she had hardly stirred from the seat of the trap except to waddle across to a comfortable stone in the Druidic Circle, from where she had watched the course of events and encouraged Lallie's bad behaviour—sank into the settee before the fire, while Hannah and Lallie busied themselves with the wild flowers of the morning, and managed to finish them off in quite a short time.

Lallie regarded her handiwork with pride.

'My Country Notebook will be pleasant to look back on later. I shall add something to it every day, if I can,' she declared, and Hannah praised her.

'Your printing of the names is beautifully done, Lallie. Why don't you also sketch some of the other flowers we see? Things that it would be difficult to press? A spray of wild roses down the side of the page, for instance?' she suggested, and Lallie seized her suggestion eagerly.

'That would make it even more interesting, wouldn't it, Miss Smith—especially if I sketched other things too—like the saint's face, and bits of scenery. What a pity I did not take my sketch-book to the Druidic Circle. Then I might have drawn some of the odd stones.'

'And the bridge across the river would make a charming study,' Hannah added.

'And some of the trees,' cried Lallie. 'There's a weeping willow further up past the house. I could do a little drawing of the leaves trailing in the water.'

She hesitated, then said very seriously: 'Miss Smith?'

'Yes, dear?' Hannah responded gently.

'I—I'm sorry for shutting you in the Mirror Room,' Lallie burst out, her face red. 'I thought you were like all the other governesses I've had—but you're not. You're different. I—I'm glad you came to us.'

'That's all right, darling, let's just forget about it, shall we?' said Hannah, feeling a surge of triumph that she had managed to break Lallie's shell and win a little of her confidence. She said nothing of the tapping on her window during her first night, nor the candles, nor the face she had seen only a few hours ago, and Lallie did not mention them. Hannah warned herself not to jump to conclusions too quickly. Lallie might be simply pretending she had been won over in order to lull Hannah's suspicions should anything further happen. The child could probably be very devious if she chose.

And as though to underline Hannah's mental warning not to feel she had won the girl over too quickly, Lallie was very offhand when she went up to bed. She did not kiss Hannah as she kissed Nanny, simply threw over her shoulder:

'Goodnight, Miss Smith.'

'Goodnight, dear. Do you want me to come with you to undo the back of your dress?' Hannah asked, and Lallie gave a shrug.

'No, I can manage.'

'Sleep well then, dear. And remember that if you want me, you only have to call, or come to my room,' Hannah said, with a smile, but Lallie did not look at her again, she simply took her candle from the row at the bottom of the stairs, and disappeared into the darkness, her little flame flickering as she went along the gallery. She had insisted, from the day they arrived at the house, that she did not want to be 'tucked in', and preferred to put herself to bed. Hannah suspected that Nanny had smothered the child with too much affection and attention when she was younger, but now, Nanny could not be bothered to climb stairs to fuss over the thirteen-year-old, and confined her hugs and kisses to saying goodnight to Lallie in the drawing-room.

Mr Armstrong did not appear again, and Hannah felt tired herself, from all the fresh air and exercise she had had that day. She sat and read for a little, then decided to go up herself. After saying goodnight to Nanny, who was dozing before the fire, Hannah took her own candelabra, and lit the candles, then climbed the stairs and went along the corridor with her skirts rustling after her.

Her mind was dwelling pleasantly on the afternoon's outing with Owen, and the thought that she would see him in a few days, and—after listening at Lallie's door and looking in briefly to find the child fast asleep—she opened the door of her own room with a light heart.

She crossed the carpet, lit her lamp, and was preparing to take the pins from her hair when suddenly she stopped and her heart leaped wildly to her throat. Something was lying on the counterpane of her bed. It was a crudely-fashioned doll with some attempt to show that it was wearing a white blouse and a long black skirt, and there was a wisp of blonde hair round the featureless face. It was obviously a representation of herself.

But it was not the crudity of the doll that made Hannah's heart suddenly cold with dread, and her knees tremble so that she had to hold onto the tallboy for support. The thing was harmless enough. What was not harmless was that someone—the person who had made the doll, she supposed—had taken one of her own hat-pins, a long one with a carved silver thistle at the end, and plunged it viciously where the doll's heart would have been, so hard that the end protruded from the back!

SIX

Hannah's first impulse was to snatch up the abominable little object—though she shrank from touching it—and rush out to confront everyone in the house, demanding to know once and for all who was playing these stupid and childish tricks on her. She was tempted to declare that she would remain no longer in a house where she was subjected to such ridiculous and malicious persecution, and to leave instantly. She could perhaps stay, she thought, with Mrs Richards until there was a suitable train for her to catch to return to London.

But as she sank down onto the padded chair in her room, her eyes fixed on the doll, she realized that this was the very reaction that the person playing the tricks was hoping for. Someone disliked her and wanted her to leave. And anger and stubbornness took the place of her fright. She would not give her persecutor the pleasure of knowing that Miss Hannah Smith had been frightened away—just as all the other governesses had. She set her mouth firmly. She would not be manipulated in such a fashion. She had come to be governess to Lallie, and governess to Lallie she would remain. But once she found out who was responsible for all this nonsense, she would certainly give them the sharp edge of her tongue—whether it was Lallie herself, Nanny, or even Mr Armstrong.

She had begun to consider who had had an opportunity to come to her room since she had left to go down to dinner, and realized that any one of the members of the household could have slipped in, placed the doll on her bed, and left unobserved. She could eliminate no-one.

After sitting and collecting herself together for some time, she decided to keep the doll, say nothing about finding it, and show it to Owen. She would also tell him about the face at the window. Perhaps his cheerful, sensible presence would be able to make some pattern out of the events that were taking place. And in the meantime, she would carry on as though nothing had happened.

Having made her decision, she took a clean handkerchief and gingerly picked up the nasty little object, wrapping it carefully. She placed it in a corner of her glove drawer, and shut the drawer firmly. Then she began to prepare for bed. But although she did not expect to fall asleep, her tiring day proved too much for her, and she slept peacefully, waking as the morning was breaking on another perfect day.

Lallie ran eagerly round the lawn the next afternoon as Mr Jones set up the croquet hoops, excitedly anticipating her game with her father. No-one had made any mention of anything out of the ordinary during the morning, and even Mair, whom Hannah had encountered in the yard while helping to fetch the croquet set, seemed to have accepted Hannah's instructions. She made no attempt to get Lallie to play with her, and bobbed a respectful courtesy as she passed Hannah, who nodded and smiled.

Yet Hannah was conscious all the time that someone—somewhere—was hiding his or her feelings very skilfully, and that she could expect further trouble. She determined to speak to Owen at the first opportunity.

Mr Armstrong's mood had switched once again, and though he remained closeted in his study during the morning, he emerged in what was for him almost a jovial frame of mind for luncheon, and teased Lallie about their croquet game, swearing that though he had not played for years, he would beat her—and Miss Smith too.

Altogether, the afternoon turned out to be a great success, Mr Armstrong complimented

Hannah on her sporting outfit of a navy-blue divided skirt and blue and white striped blouse, and seemed a different person when he smiled at her. She could hardly believe that it was he who was tormenting her with foolish tricks, and she responded to his compliments, so that they almost seemed like friends, while Lallie, delighted at further attention from her father, bloomed as she knocked the ball everywhere but through the hoops.

When one of her efforts sent it spinning out onto the river, where it floated away, everyone thought the episode the greatest joke possible, and even Mr Armstrong laughed whole-heartedly. Hannah thought that part of their enjoyment might be due to the absence of Nanny, who had decided to spend the afternoon dozing on the drawing-room settee. She could not help feeling that Nanny, with her silly superstitions and her doting on Lallie, whom she still persisted as regarding as a child, had a dampening effect, and she wished that Mr Armstrong would pension Nanny off. So far as she could see, Nanny was little use about the house at all. But of course, she did not dare to suggest it to him.

Another ball was produced, and the game continued, and it was a flushed and breathless little party that trooped in to tidy themselves up for tea.

Mr Armstrong stopped Hannah in the hall, and took her arm.

'Thank you, Miss Smith,' he said, his dark eyes intent on hers. 'I think perhaps the sky has seemed blue for me for a few hours today.'

'Lallie does enjoy your company so much, sir,' Hannah told him, adding impulsively: 'And so do I.'

'Do you?' he asked, slowly, and she nodded.

'Yes, sir, I do.' Emboldened by his good humour, she could not help adding: 'Mrs Richard's invitation for you to accompany us to tea on Thursday still stands, sir. Do you think—?'

But his mood changed as though a summer storm had blown up, and his face darkened.

'No!' he said explosively and, without another word, he turned on his heel and left her. Hannah sighed. What an unpredictable man he was!

Lallie had become absorbed in her Country Notebook, and happily pottered around the next day making little sketches to decorate it with, and taking great pains to do a spray of wild roses in water colours. Hannah could tell, however, that she was really waiting eagerly to show it to her father and win his approval. She suspected that the completed project would be presented to Mr Armstrong when they returned to London, for since Mr Armstrong had begun to take an interest in his daughter's doings, Lallie's thoughts were all on her father and his attention.

His mood changed yet again, and on

Wednesday evening, he sat down after dinner with Lallie to inspect her efforts, and appeared genuinely interested.

'Yes, Lalage, you must certainly develop this talent of yours for drawing,' he commented, after studying her sketch of the weeping willow trailing its leaves in the water of the river. 'And the little flowers—' He gave one of his rare smiles. 'They'll bring the countryside right into the heart of Belgravia.'

'You do like it then, Papa?' demanded Lallie, flushed with pride at his praise.

'I think it's a most admirable effort. A real work of art,' said her father. 'I did not imagine I possessed such a talented daughter.'

Lallie looked down at her feet, overcome.

'It was really Miss Smith's idea,' she said generously, and Mr Armstrong looked across to where Hannah was sitting quietly doing some needlework.

'Yes, Miss Smith has made a real difference in our lives,' he said, and for a moment, she recalled her dream and the note of tenderness she had put into his voice in her imagination. She flushed.

'Perhaps, as a grand opening to the book you could do a sketch of the house itself, Lallie,' she suggested, and Lallie screwed up her face with thought.

'From the bridge, I think,' she pondered. 'Then I should be able to get everything in, even the trees at the back.'

110

'You do not draw or paint, Miss Smith?' enquired Mr Armstrong, leaning back in his chair, and Hannah shook her head with a smile.

'Only enough to be able to get by socially, sir,' she answered. 'I prefer to read. And I love playing the pianoforte.'

'It would be pleasant to hear you, but I am afraid we have no pianoforte here—with the house being shut-up so often, I fear an instrument would go out of tune, being used so little,' said Mr Armstrong. 'Can you sing, Miss Smith?'

'I love singing, sir. Especially if I can accompany myself,' said Hannah, and he asked:

'Will you sing for us now?'

'Unaccompanied, sir?' asked Hannah.

'Why not? A lovely voice is not less lovely because it sings alone,' said Mr Armstrong, and Hannah began to hum softly to herself, then, with no pretence at a real performance, she sang the old English ballad 'Greensleeves', while the others listened—except for Nanny, who had dozed off to sleep as usual in front of the fire.

'Oh, Miss Smith, that was beautiful,' cried Lallie, when she had finished, and she clapped her hands. 'Another!'

So Hannah began 'Come into the garden, Maud', and was both surprised and pleased when Mr Armstrong joined in, his rich

111

baritone blending harmoniously with her own voice. She stopped singing to listen, and it seemed to her as though he sang with some deeper meaning than convention demanded. As though he was singing for her alone. She recalled her dream again, and blushed.

'Sir, you have a—an admirable voice,' she said, when he brought the song to a lingering conclusion, his eyes on her.

'And so do you, Miss Smith,' he declared, with another of his rare smiles.

Something hovered in the air, something delicate and fragile, but before Hannah could decide what it was, or try to capture it, Nanny snuffled in her sleep, and the spell was broken.

Lallie was yawning, and Hannah, recollecting her duties, said: 'Bedtime, Lallie. Ring the bell for Angharad to bring your hot milk, dear, will you?'

As Lallie drank her nightcap, Mr Armstrong rose.

'I will say goodnight too, Miss Smith,' he declared, and added seemingly casually: 'I hope that one day, I may have the pleasure of singing duets with you, with a real pianoforte accompaniment.'

'That would be very pleasant, sir,' said Hannah, going pink again, though she could not have said why. Mr Armstrong turned to Lallie.

'Goodnight, Lalage,' he said, with more gentleness and affection than he had ever

112

displayed towards his daughter before, and Lallie hesitated, on the verge of throwing her arms about him, Hannah could see. But she hesitated just that fraction of a second too long, and her father had turned away before she could move.

'Goodnight, Papa,' she cried warmly.

When he had gone, Hannah came across and took Lallie's hand.

'Don't worry, dear. Some time your Papa will be able to hug you and hold you the way you want him to. But he is—he is not an easy man to get to know, and you must be patient,' she said softly.

'He never took any notice of me at all before we came here,' said Lallie. 'I think you are a witch, Miss Smith. He seems like a different person. But I know he has a temper, and I don't want to upset him.'

'Just be yourself, darling, and he'll come to love you as you are. He is trying very hard, but it is not easy for him after so many years of being shut up alone with his books,' Hannah reassured her.

Just before Lallie went upstairs, she said: 'Imagine, Miss Smith. I never heard Papa sing before tonight. Never.'

And she was gone, leaving Hannah with thoughts that were both confused and pleasurable.

*   *   *

The following afternoon, Hannah made an occasion of the fact that they were going out on a social call, and Lallie spent quite half-an-hour trying to decide which of her dresses to wear. Eventually she decided on a plain white one with a low waist, made of broiderie anglaise, with frills round the shoulders in a square pattern. She wore blue-buttoned boots and Hannah did her hair in a long braid, and tied it with a matching blue ribbon.

'There! Now you look like a real young lady going out to call on someone for tea,' she said, as she smoothed Lallie's dark glossy hair into place. 'Don't dirty the dress, while I get ready, will you, dear?'

'I'm going to sit in the drawing-room and put all the sketches I did this morning in order,' Lallie responded, and went off down the passage, while Hannah returned to her own room to dress.

She washed in the hot water the girls had brought up, and slipped on a tea-gown in a deceptively simple style in white crepe-de-chine. With her suede shoes and her hair piled up beneath a big white hat, she thought she looked both discreet yet elegant, and anticipated that Owen would admire her—a thought that pleased her. Not so governessy this afternoon, she decided, pleasurably regarding her reflection in the mirror.

A white parasol completed her outfit, lined

with pink silk so that if she opened it, a rosy glow was cast over her. And the day was fine and sunny, so she thought she might have reason to open it if she and Owen managed to get away into the garden, say, to talk alone.

Into her small white bag she put the horrible little doll, still wrapped in her handkerchief. She wanted very much to tell Owen about that, and the face she had seen at the window, and hoped she would have a chance to speak with him alone.

Downstairs, as the trap was being brought round, she sent Lallie up for her own blue hat, a velvet affair with a big bow that matched her boots and ribbon, and they waited on the steps for Mr Jones to turn the pony in the drive.

'Two young ladies off for tea,' Hannah smiled. 'You look very charming, Lallie dear. We shall have to invite Mrs Richards and Dr Owen here for tea in return.'

'I've brought my sketch-book. Mrs Richards might have some unusual flowers in her garden,' responded Lallie, accepting the compliment in an offhand way, though Hannah could tell she was pleased. 'And I think I saw a rose arbour outside the doctor's house when we went to the village. I'd like to draw that.'

'I'm sure Mrs Richards will be only too pleased to let you draw whatever you like.' Hannah said, glad that Lallie might be diverted from herself and Owen. 'Well, here

115

we are. Into the trap you go. Take care with your dress.'

So they were driven off in style to the village, and Mrs Richards was waiting for them at the gate, with Owen at her side.

'My, my, what visions of delight!' exclaimed Owen, with his rugged smile. 'Miss Lalage, may I assist you to alight?'

Lallie's cheeks were a delighted pink as he handed her down from the trap with aplomb, and Hannah followed, to find Mrs Richards taking her hand.

'How good to see you, my dear. I thought we would have tea in the garden, it's such a lovely day,' she declared, and Lallie, hearing the words, could hardly contain herself. Tea in the garden was a treat for her.

Mr Jones was told when to call back for them, and he drove away, leaving the two to wander with Mrs Richards and Owen up the rustic path between the flowers. Lallie exclaimed with delight at the various blooms, and chattered happily to Mrs Richards about her Country Sketchbook, while Owen hung back to have a word with Hannah.

'You look like a queen,' he declared. 'I wish I dared to kiss your hand, but I'm afraid I might get my cheek slapped.' And he rubbed his face ruefully.

Hannah did not laugh.

'I'd like to talk to you—alone,' she said beneath her breath. 'Something very strange

116

has happened, and I'd value your opinion. Something quite—well, frightening.'

'After tea, when Lallie is sketching her flowers. Mother will keep out of the way if I drop a hint,' Owen said seriously. 'You're all right, though aren't you? You haven't been hurt?'

Hannah shook her head.

'Oh, no, it's just that—some more of those odd happenings have occurred. Someone at the house is trying to frighten me away. I don't know who. Lallie seems to have accepted me, but still—I can't be sure it isn't all pretence. And Mr Armstrong's behaviour is quite unpredictable. Sometimes he is friendly, and other times, he seems to be sneering at me. Then there's Nanny—I'm not at all sure she wouldn't like me out of the way—'

There was no time to say more, for Lallie came rushing up to tell them of the wonderful things she had found to sketch. And when they turned the corner of the house and saw the table set on the lawn, she clasped her hands ecstatically.

'Oh, I must draw a picture called "Tea on the Lawn",' she cried. 'And look, Miss Smith, what we are having to eat—oh, I do love chocolate cake! And jelly!'

The happy group seated themselves round the table, and Mrs Richards' little maid came hurrying out with the silver tea-service on a tray. Mrs Richards poured the tea in frail

117

china cups, which fascinated Lallie because they were painted both inside and out with exotic dragons, and rimmed with gold.

'Have they come all the way from China?' she asked eagerly, and Mrs Richards smiled.

'Yes, dear, they have. One of my ancestors was a sailor, and he brought them back in a clipper ship, with huge white sails. That was before they had invented the steamships of today, and railway trains, and such things.'

She kept Lallie fascinated with stories while they drank their tea and ate the dainty sandwiches and the cake—and the jelly, which had obviously been provided especially for Lallie's benefit.

'I asked Mr Armstrong if he would like to come with us, but I'm afraid he was no more sociable than on other occasions,' Hannah told her hostess, who looked more than ever like a porcelain figurine in a soft pink tea-gown with many ruffles, a little lace cap on her pale hair. The tree above their table cast green and gold shadows across her delicate white skin.

'But you must come to tea with us,' Lallie interposed, grandly. 'We will have it out-of-doors too—beside the river.'

'How delightful. We should be charmed, should we not, Owen?' smiled Mrs Richards, and Lallie declared: 'So that is settled. Will you come next week?'

'I think our social round is sufficiently leisurely for me to be able to say that we can

118

come any time you wish,' Mrs Richards told her, adding: 'Providing someone does not break a leg or decide to have a baby just as we are setting out. Owen is liable to be summoned at any time of the day to attend to a sick person.'

'But strangely enough, most of my calls come during the night,' Owen said ruefully. 'I think people do it deliberately, just as I think my calls are over for the day, in order to make sure I never have any sleep.'

Lallie laughed delightedly, and they continued to chat until they had finished tea, when Mrs Richards suggested that perhaps the girl would like to do a little sketching.

'I'll come with you and tell you about the flowers as you draw them. We'll leave these two old fuddy-duddies to sit and gossip,' she said, and Lallie reached for her sketch-book and pencil. Soon she and Mrs Richards were happily absorbed in their task.

'Now,' Owen said to Hannah, as his mother and Lallie disappeared round the corner of the house, and Hannah opened her bag with trembling fingers, and drew out the little doll, which she handed to him.

'Someone left this on my bed,' she told him, and he unwrapped the handkerchief, and grimaced as he looked at the vicious little object.

'Hannah! This is not funny. It's—ghoulish.'

'Yes, there is something malicious about it,

119

I felt that,' Hannah said, troubled, and she told him about the face she had seen in the mirror, Caroline's face, appearing outside her window.

'And you could find no trace of where it had come from?' he asked thoughtfully.

She shrugged.

'It had obviously been let down on a string from the window above my own. I made enquiries, and found that the room in question is shut-up and not used, though it isn't locked. Anyone could have done it. I was alone in my room and I don't know where the others were during those few moments, though I think Lallie was innocent. She was fastening her dress when I went in, and that's quite a difficult task with all the hooks up the back. Nanny was in her room, and she didn't seem to have hurried back from anywhere, she was finishing doing her hair. That only leaves Mr Armstrong—but why would he want to play a trick like that on me? Sometimes I begin to wonder if his mind has not been warped by his wife's death, so that he—well, does things for no apparent reason, or is not even aware that he is doing them.'

'Whoever made this doll and left it in your bed had gone to a lot of trouble. They certainly knew what they were doing all right,' Owen said grimly. 'The hat-pin—'

'It's one of my own,' Hannah told him. 'It was on my dressing-table, in the trinket tray.'

Owen debated for a moment, then he said:

'Leave that house, Hannah. I—well, I wouldn't have said anything just yet, but—ever since I saw you in the lane—you have been in my thoughts. Is it too soon for me to say that—?'

Sensing what was coming, Hannah stopped him with a gesture.

'Yes, I think things have happened too quickly,' she said, and looked into his eyes. 'I know what you are going to say, but—I will not be frightened away by petty tyranny. And as for—the other—I—my feelings are so confused just at the moment, I don't really know what I think.'

'I want to be more than just a friend to you, my dear,' Owen said gently. 'Will you remember that? Will you consider what I could offer you? It is not a great deal, but—life here is leisurely and pleasant, and there could surely be no more beautiful place to live. I—will not speak again of my feelings. This is not the time, as you have said, to tell you what is in my heart. Except to say that as soon as I saw you, I seemed to lose that particular part of my anatomy. It is in your keeping, my love. And has been since the moment I set my eyes on you.'

'I am—deeply honoured, Owen, truly, but you must understand, I need time to think,' Hannah said, averting her gaze. It would be so easy to accept this strange, unorthodox proposal, and live her life out here as the wife of a country doctor. Yet something held her

121

back. Something drew her to Bethel House, she did not know what. She told herself it was Lallie, that she was becoming fond of the child, but it was something more than that, something she did not even want to recognize.

It was perhaps fortunate that Lallie herself came round the corner at that moment, crying: 'Dr Owen! Dr Owen! I had forgotten all about Henry! You must let me see Henry.'

'Ah, yes, Henry,' said Owen, rising. 'Well, let's go into the house and you shall inspect him in all his glory. Miss Hannah, would you care to accompany us?'

Mrs Richards showed Hannah the comfortable, peaceful rooms of the house while Lallie exclaimed over the fleshless Henry, and Owen made the bones of the skeleton rattle for her.

'I still can't make up my mind if he was really alive once,' Lallie said consideringly. 'Was he, doctor?'

'I'm not telling. I told you you would have to guess,' Owen said solemnly, and Lallie touched the bones.

'Is that what we all look like inside?' she demanded.

'Indeed it is, my dear young lady. Although perhaps not quite so handsome as Henry,' Owen said, and Lallie drew a breath.

'Imagine!' she exclaimed, then declared with some bravado: 'Well, I don't think he was ever real at all. I think he was made.'

'For the guidance of Medical School students,' agreed Owen.

'I'd like to have a Henry too. I shall ask Papa to buy one for me, and I'll hang him in my room so that if anyone bad comes in when I am asleep, they'll be frightened away,' Lallie said, and Owen and Hannah exchanged glances, thinking of the little doll and the face at the window.

All too soon, it seemed, Mr Jones arrived with the trap, and the visit was over.

'But don't forget, you are coming to tea with us next week. A week today—on Thursday,' Lallie reminded her host and hostess as they said goodbye, and they all exchanged smiles and waves, as the trap moved away. Owen blew a kiss in the air after them, and Hannah looked down at her gloved hands. She knew the kiss was meant for her.

*   *   *

That evening, after Mr Armstrong, who was in one of his unapproachable moods, had retired to his study after dinner, the talk came round to birthdays, and Lallie revealed that her father's birthday fell the following Saturday.

'Why—we should celebrate the event,' said Hannah, once again seeking a way to bring father and daughter together. 'Let me think! I have it! We'll hold a dinner-party especially for your Papa, Lallie.'

123

'But he always has dinner with us,' Lallie said in some bewilderment, and Hannah explained:

'No, no, I meant we'd have a really special dinner, and you shall be the hostess and invite us all. We'll send him and Nanny invitations, shall we? You can write them out in that lovely clear script you have, and we'll make it obvious that this is to be a really Grand Occasion. We'll all put on our evening dress—the grandest we have—and your Papa shall be the guest of honour.'

'Oh! Do you think he'll like that?' asked Lallie, with round eyes, and Hannah said:

'Well, we can try it, can't we? Come along, let's make out the invitations now.'

So invitations were duly written by Lallie, with much concentration on her task, inviting Mr Gervaise Armstrong and Nanny to a Dinner Party on Saturday evening in honour of Mr Armstrong's birthday. While Lallie did the invitations, Hannah prepared an exotic menu of seven courses.

Then Hannah directed: 'Now slip the invitations one beneath your Papa's study door, Lallie, and the other one on Nanny's pillow so that she will see it when she goes to bed. And since we have asked them to reply, we will know tomorrow what their answer is to be.'

The following day, Lallie was in a fever of excitement. Nanny came down full of garbled

124

wonder at the prospect of a Dinner Party, and did not quite understand what it was all about, so Lallie had to explain it to her. Then Mr Armstrong entered the room. He was holding a white envelope in his hand, and without a word, he presented it to Lallie with a bow.

She breathlessly opened it, and read out:

'Mr Gervaise Armstrong is happy to accept the invitation to the Dinner Party to be held on Saturday next in honour of his birthday, and presents his compliments to Miss Lalage Armstrong.' Then, with a radiant face, she looked up at her father. 'Oh, Papa! Are you pleased? Really? We have the most delicious menu—Miss Smith devised it—and we are going to make this a really Grand Occasion.'

'I did observe that 'Dress will be worn',' Mr Armstrong remarked drily. 'Don't worry, I won't let the side down, Lalage. Though it is some time since I have attended a Dinner Party.'

'Of course, there will only be the four of us,' Lallie babbled on happily and, suddenly, she threw her arms round her father, and gave him a quick hug, before darting away, overcome at her own daring. He watched her go with a strange expression in his eyes. He really loves her, thought Hannah, delighted at the success of her plan. They are becoming closer all the time.

And it was on a wave of exultation that she followed Lallie from the room.

SEVEN

That night, Hannah did not sleep for a long time. She lay, thinking over the events of the afternoon—and especially the fact that she had received her first proposal! A proposal of marriage! She had always wondered who it would be—and how it would be—and she could think of no-one more sympathetic and likeable than the rugged Welshman. Though she had known him for so short a time, she respected and admired Owen, and admitted rather wistfully that his wife would be a lucky woman indeed.

But—here she turned upon her pillow—could she honestly say she was in love with Owen? That she wished to spend the rest of her life with him—even though in such a charming part of the country? Something deep within her stirred regretfully as her innate self-honesty forced her to admit that something was missing—some spark that she wanted in a romance. The trouble was that her dream about Mr Armstrong had shown her she was capable of strong, wild passions, and if ever he, for instance, should behave as he had behaved in her dream—

But that was nonsense! Mr Armstrong felt nothing for her except perhaps an unwilling admiration for her capabilities. And she? What

126

did she feel for him? She told herself firmly that she did *not* love her employer—that he was a moody and selfish man—that he would bring heartbreak to any woman who happened to be so unfortunate as to fall in love with him. And yet—the man in her dream had been so different—gentle and tender, but with a fierce passion that had sparked off an involuntary response in her. She could not help it, but the dark masterful face of her dream swam before her and blotted out Owen's blond image.

Hannah's thoughts went round and round in a circle, until at last, she drifted into a daze. A whisper awoke her some time later.

'Hannah! Hannah!'

She opened her eyes in the darkness, and lifted her head. Had she dreamed those softly-spoken words? But no—they came again, from the direction of her door.

'Hannah! Hannah! Come! Come with me!'

'Who is it? Is that you, Lallie?' Hannah said aloud, her eyes straining to pierce the gloom. 'Who's there?'

'Caroline,' the voice whispered, and Hannah felt her whole body turn cold as ice.

'I'm going to light the lamp,' she said, and the voice stopped her as she was sitting up to reach for the matches.

'No! No lamp! Come with me, Hannah! I have something to show you.'

'I can't see in the dark,' said Hannah, and found she was trembling. Chills were running up her spine and down the backs of her legs, along her exposed arms.

'Follow me! I will guide you,' the voice whispered. 'Come now. Along the corridor to the gallery. Then you shall know everything.'

Hannah's teeth were chattering, and she clamped them firmly together. She was not going to be frightened. Perhaps Caroline Armstrong was not dead—perhaps she had never died in Switzerland, as everyone believed. Perhaps she was shut-up here in this house—

'Why can't I light the lamp?' she demanded into the darkness, and the voice answered:

'You must not see me as I am now. Don't be afraid. Just walk along the corridor to the gallery, and down the stairs. I will go ahead. Come—come now—now—'

The whisper was fading, and Hannah was torn between lighting her lamp and perhaps revealing some horror. Caroline might be disfigured—hideous—But she had promised that all would be revealed if Hannah went along to the gallery and down the stairs. Quickly, without even trying to find her robe in the darkness, Hannah slipped out of bed and made her cautious way to the door. It was standing ajar. She pushed it open, and the blackness of the corridor met her gaze, deep and impenetrable.

'Caroline?' she said tentatively.

'I'm here,' the voice whispered from the end

128

of the passage. 'This way, Hannah.'

As though in a dream, but drawn by some irresistible force, Hannah groped her way along the panels of the corridor, until she reached the end, and the turn to the gallery. She moved on round the comer. Still all was dark, but starlight filtered through the windows on each side of the huge front door, revealing a shape that moved at the top of the stairs.

'Come, Hannah,' the shadowy figure whispered. 'Come to me. Don't be afraid.'

'Who are you? Are you really Caroline? Are you not dead?' Hannah found that her voice was trembling.

'Soon you will know everything,' the figure promised. 'Come—down the stairs—'

Hannah went slowly along the gallery, to the shape that waited. As she reached the dim outline of the figure, she smelled a familiar fragrance, which took her a moment to identify. It was lily-of-the-valley.

'Now go down the stairs,' the voice urged, while the figure stood a few feet from Hannah, just out of her reach, Hannah strained her eyes, but the starlight showed her only a woman's shape with a sort of veil over her head and face. Feeling as though she was in the middle of a nightmare, she turned and took two careful steps down the stairs, holding onto the bannister.

Then two things happened simultaneously.

129

Hannah felt a violent push from behind in the middle of her back, and as she fell forward, her feet caught in some sort of obstacle. She completely lost her balance, and went head-first down the stairs into blackness, her hands flailing the air, and the sound of someone screaming filling her ears. She did not realize that it was herself. Her hands caught at nothing, but her knees and feet bumped painfully against the edges of the stairs, there was a sudden stabbing pain in her ankle, and then her head crashed against the floor of the hall, and she sank into an even deeper darkness of nothingness.

*   *   *

Voices came and went in her ears, and lights made her head ache even though her eyes were shut against them. She had a fleeting sensation of strong arms enfolding her and of her body being lifted. She felt comforted and safe, even in her pain. But the next time she surfaced to awareness, the comforting arms were gone, and she was lying down on something soft, warm, something that should have been comfortable, but was not, for her whole being seemed to ache, her ankle was throbbing, and her head felt as though a hundred hammers were beating in her brain.

A far-away voice came to her.

'There, there, cariad, not to worry, the

doctor's been sent for. She's coming round, sir.'

Another voice that she thought vaguely was Mr Armstrong's demanded, and to Hannah's amazement, there was passionate anxiety in it: 'But she is going to be all right? If she fell from the top, there might be internal injuries—concussion—how on earth could such a thing have happened?'

She summoned all her strength and managed to whisper: 'It—was—Caroline—she pushed me—'

There was a silence, then the voices spoke again, in muted tones.

'Could she be delirious? Has she a fever, Mrs Jones?'

'No, sir. Probably she was dreaming. Bruises and cuts, a bad ankle, and she'll have a nasty head for a few days, but there's no fever.'

'It was Caroline,' Hannah tried to tell them, but a hand soothed her aching head with a moistened cloth, and Mrs Jones crooned:

'There, there, cariad, rest easy now. The doctor will be here in a minute. Caroline's been dead these ten years. It was a dream.'

'No—' Hannah protested weakly, tears of frustration coming to her eyes and running down her cheeks into the pillow. 'You—must believe me—she called to me—she told me to go down the stairs, and then—she pushed me—and there was something in the way of my feet—'

The sound of other voices approaching, and the door opening reached Hannah's ears, and Mrs Jones said, with relief: 'Here we are, then, here's Dr Richards. He'll soon put you right.'

Hannah managed to open her eyes and Owen's face swam dizzily into her view. He took her hand.

'Now then, Hannah, what have you been doing to yourself? Sleepwalking? Falling down the stairs? I can't trust you out of my sight for a minute, can I?'

'It was—Caroline, Owen,' she whispered, with an effort, clinging to his hand. 'She came—in the night—and told me to follow her—and then she pushed me down the stairs—'

'Well, well, we'll sort that out later my dear. The main thing is to make you comfortable, and see that you have a good rest,' Owen said, his gentle, capable hands disengaging from hers, and feeling her in a professional manner for broken bones. He took her pulse, looked at her ankle, and moved it very gently, and then said in a calm voice to Mrs Jones, who had remained in the room during the examination:

'I'll need a cold water compress for that ankle. It's a bad sprain, that's all, fortunately. And then bring hot water for me to see to the cut and bruise on her head. There's a good deal of blood clotted in her hair, and a nasty gash on her scalp. Where's my bag?' Hannah submitted listlessly to his ministrations, and the fussing of Mrs Jones. Nobody believed her. But she knew, she *knew* she had not dreamed the voice that had called to her, she *knew* that Caroline, or someone masquerading as Caroline, had lured her from her room and then actually threatened her very life. For if her unknown enemy had been harmless before, Hannah could see clearly that he or she did not intend to remain harmless for ever.

No, her life was in danger. She might have broken her neck on the stairs—or at the very least, suffered some severe injury that could have left her paralyzed, permanently damaged in some way. Hannah could only conclude, in her bemused state, that her enemy either hated her very much, or was mad. That was the only answer to the puzzling question of 'who'? She decided that, once she had recovered herself somewhat, and Owen did not believe she was wandering in a delirious manner, she would tell him everything, calmly and coolly. He would listen then, she was sure, and would be able to advise her.

When he had finished his ministrations, Hannah felt distinctly better. Her ankle no longer throbbed so agonizingly, her head was easier, and he gave her something on a spoon and said disarmingly: 'Come on, Hannah, you've been a very brave patient. Now drink this, like a good girl.'

Obediently, Hannah swallowed the liquid, which had quite a pleasant taste, and he tucked her back among her pillows.

'Now go to sleep, my dear,' he said softly. 'I'll come again in the morning.'

Hannah managed to smile at him, as drowsiness overcame her.

'I'm sorry I called you out—in the middle of the—night—' she whispered, before his face dissolved into a gentle mist of blackness. She slept.

*　　　*　　　*

The medication ensured that Hannah slept like a child until Owen arrived the next morning, and she was just beginning to recover her wits and take pleasure in the sunlight outside her windows, where the curtains had been drawn back, and finish the bowl of broth, rich with vegetables, that Mrs Jones had brought her on a tray, when a knock at the door announced his presence.

He came in, smiling.

'There's a very anxious young lady who has been on tenterhooks to see our patient ever since she fell in the night. She's waiting patiently outside,' he said, and Hannah cried:

'Lallie! Oh, poor darling. Of course I must see her.'

'I'll tell her she can come in. I can see that you are very much better this morning,' Owen said, with his rugged smile and, a few seconds later, Lallie came rushing through the door and almost threw herself on top of Hannah, hugging her tightly with her thin arms.

'Oh, Miss Smith! Are you better? They wouldn't let me see you in the night, I only knew that something bad had happened to you, although Papa was—well, he sat with me until I went back to sleep, and told me over and over that you would be better in the morning,' she burst out. 'Are you really better now?'

'Yes, dear, I'm almost as good as new,' Hannah said reassuringly, kissing the top of Lallie's head. She could be certain of one thing—Lallie had not been the figure she had seen in the night—she was not tall enough, and the poor child was obviously genuinely anxious about her governess.

'Will you be better in time for our Grand Dinner Party tomorrow evening?' Lallie enquired, her huge brown eyes solemn. 'I—I don't want Papa to be disappointed, you see,' she went on, and Hannah deduced that her accident and Mr Armstrong's patience with the troubled child had brought the two even closer together.

'Certainly. I intend to get up when all this fuss is over—even if I have to sit on the settee for the rest of the day,' Hannah declared vigorously. 'It was nothing really, Lallie, just a bang on the head and a sprained ankle, dear. Wasn't I silly to go wandering about in the dark and fall down the stairs? Next time I must make sure I have my lamp or candle with me.'

Lallie quite obviously felt much easier in her mind about the whole affair.

'When you get up, I'll come and sit with you, and we'll play some quiet game, or I'll draw you—I'd like to draw you,' she said, and Owen appeared to indicate that he would now like to see the patient. Mrs Jones hovered determinedly in the background, a model chaperone.

'I'll see you later on, Miss Smith,' said Lallie, and Hannah responded:

'Yes, darling. You go along now, while the doctor tells me I can get up.'

Lallie skipped from the room, her face cleared of anxiety, and Owen grinned at Hannah.

'And what if the doctor says you can't get up, young lady? A day resting in bed would do both your head and ankle the world of good, you know.'

'It's no use, Owen,' Hannah said determinedly. 'I can't disappoint Lallie now that I've told her I'm getting up. I'll rest on the settee all day, if that will please you. But truly, I feel much, much better. My head is quite clear, and my ankle hardly hurts at all.'

'Just wait until you try walking on it. I think you'd better be carried about today,' said Owen, seriously. 'Now, let me have a proper look at your leg and your head.'

He examined Hannah's ankle, renewed the

bandages, and replaced the dressing on her head.

'Well, I think you'll live. But don't go falling down any more stairs,' he said, washing his hands in the bowl of water Mrs Jones was holding after he had finished.

'Owen,' Hannah said urgently. 'I must talk to you—alone.'

She was sitting up in her nightdress and green chiffon robe, and Owen turned to Mrs Jones.

'Thank you. Would you leave us for a while, Mrs Jones?'

Mrs Jones gave Hannah a sceptical glance, then left the room. Owen sat down on Hannah's bed, and took her hand.

'What is it, dearest?'

'I know I must have sounded crazy last night,' Hannah began carefully, without looking at him. 'But I've told you about the strange things that have happened, and this was another of them, Owen, I swear it. I wasn't dreaming, and I wasn't walking in my sleep.' She looked full into his face. 'It all happened just as I said. Someone came to my door, and called very softly to wake me, and said she was Caroline. I was going to light the lamp, but she told me not to, and instructed me to follow her to the stairs, and she said I would soon know everything. Then, when I reached the top of the stairs, she bade me go down, and as I started down, she—or someone else—gave

137

me a violet push in the middle of my back, and there was something across the stairs—a rope, or a cord of some sort—that caught my feet—and that was how I came to fall. That is the truth. I swear it.'

Owen was looking serious.

'But this means that you are no longer safe in this house, Hannah,' he said in concern. 'You might have been killed. Oh, my darling—' and he gathered her into his arms. 'You might have broken your back—broken your neck. I can't let you stay here.' He was kissing her face passionately, and dazedly, Hannah responded, thankful that he believed her, and grateful for his protective love.

'I asked you to marry me—not in so many words—and I am asking you again,' Owen urged, his hands moving over her body, pushing aside the chiffon robe. 'Oh, my love—my sweet beautiful Hannah—you care for me too, don't you? Not just as a friend? Say you do. It's torment to have you in my arms like this—to be able to touch you—'

'Owen—dear Owen—' Hannah whispered, swept away for the moment by his passion. His lips were on her hair, her neck, and he pushed the straps of her nightdress to one side, and buried his face in her breasts. Hannah tried weakly to push him away, but her body was stirring with langorous feelings such as she had never before experienced in her life. She whispered dazedly:

'Owen—no—this is not right—'

'Yes, my darling, it is,' he urged, his hands on her skin, while his lips sought her mouth again. His kisses made her head swirl, and once more she made a feeble attempt to pull away.

'I—Owen, stop—I feel dizzy—'

'This is love, my darling,' he said huskily, and she shut her eyes, trembling.

'Owen—no—oh, no—'

His shirt was open, and his strong chest against her breasts as he held her in a tight embrace. Then, without warning, the door opened, and Mr Armstrong strode in. He stood aghast, while Owen leaped hastily from the bed, pulling his shirt closed, and Hannah, blushing furiously, seized a sheet and pulled it to her chin.

For a long moment, there was silence, then Mr Armstrong stated emotionlessly:

'Forgive me for interrupting, doctor, Miss Smith. I understood from Mrs Jones that the patient required to be carried down to rest on the settee, and came to offer my services. I can see that they will not be required. Obviously you can both manage without my assistance.'

'Sir,' Owen blurted, with as much dignity as he could muster under the circumstances. 'I have asked Miss Smith to be my wife.'

'And she, apparently, has no objection to anticipating her marriage night,' Mr Armstrong said, his lip curling.

Hannah was almost in tears.

'I—Owen—I tried to stop him, but—'

'Did you dare to violate Miss Smith against her will?' Mr Armstrong demanded, his face like a thundercloud as he glared at Owen. 'You are a disgrace to your profession, doctor. Miss Smith, have you agreed to marry Dr Richards?'

'No—' Hannah faltered, and Mr Armstrong seized Owen by the arm, and pushed his jacket and medical bag into his hands, then hustled him to the door.

'I never want to see you in this house again, sir,' he said, in a low, furious voice, and with a helpless look at Hannah, Owen disappeared.

Mr Armstrong turned to Hannah.

'You should have called for assistance, Miss Smith.'

'I—it was not altogether his fault—I look on him as a friend—we were talking—and things just—happened,' Hannah faltered. 'I fear I must take some of the blame, sir. I—I just don't know what happened to me. He was so gentle—so—so—'

She stopped, unable to continue and, to her horror, tears of weakness and shame that he should have witnessed her in such a situation came to her eyes.

'He loves me,' she sobbed. 'I could not be harsh to him.'

'And you love him?' Mr Armstrong asked, his arms folded, as he turned his back on her

140

and looked out of the window.

'I—don't know,' Hannah managed, and then broke down completely. He came across immediately, and offered her a clean white handkerchief.

'You have had a very upsetting night, and he took advantage of your weakness,' he said; but to Hannah, he sounded as though he was trying to convince himself, not her. He sat down on the edge of the bed in his turn, and when he spoke, his voice was gentle.

'If I withdraw for you to attire yourself in suitable garments, Miss Smith, would you like me to carry you down to the settee? We will have to forget that this upsetting scene ever occurred. Although I find it hard to forgive that—that blackguard!'

'Thank you, sir,' said Hannah, her head bent, and he left the room. She pulled on her nightdress and her green chiffon robe, tying the sash firmly about her waist. Lallie would be waiting for her, and it was no good lying here brooding.

When she was ready, she called to Mr Armstrong, and he lifted her carefully, and proceeded to carry her down the stairs to the drawing-room, where he settled her on the settee and made sure she was comfortable. She recognized those arms, she thought, with a quickening of her heart. They were the arms that had carried her to safety after she had fallen down the stairs.

He seemed extra gentle and protective, and she was emboldened to ask hesitantly:

'Sir—I wonder—I am sure you will think this a foolish question, but did your wife—did Caroline really die? I was not dreaming last night, and if it was not Caroline who summoned me from my bed, it was someone masquerading as her—someone who wishes me harm. Other—odd events have occurred since I arrived here, but until last night, nothing that could be interpreted as intending harm towards me. Just—malicious and foolish pranks.'

Mr Armstrong's brows came together.

'I can assure you, Miss Smith, that my wife is certainly and undoubtedly deceased these ten years,' he replied, and went on: 'What do you mean by 'foolish pranks'?'

'Oh—faces appearing at my window—nothing to trouble you with, sir,' Hannah said hastily.

'Last night's incident was not a foolish prank, Miss Smith,' he said sternly. 'I would have been inclined to dismiss your presence on the stairs as due to sleepwalking or something of the sort, if it were not for the fact that I know you are a young lady of extreme commonsense and not inclined to be hysterical—as Lalage's other governesses have been. None of them ever suffered personal injury, but this is something quite different. You say you think the person who lured you from your room may have been masquerading as Caroline. Have you any idea at all who it could have been?'

Hannah moved her hands helplessly.

'No, sir,' she admitted. 'But I can only conclude that the—person in question either hates me very much, or else is—well, to put it bluntly, sir, insane. I can think of no-one whom I have offended to any degree that they would wish me dead, and you yourself would be certain to know if any member of the household was insane.'

He frowned.

'I must think over what you have said, Miss Smith. I admit that I am deeply disturbed. You might have been seriously injured—or indeed, have been killed, as you yourself pointed out. You must be on your guard from this moment on. I presume—' He hesitated, then continued: 'I presume that you do not wish to leave us as a result of last night's occurrence?'

There was something in his face—some fleeting and indefinable expression in his eyes—that made Hannah, who had indeed been considering leaving Bethel House, speak impulsively.

'Not if you wish me to stay, sir.'

'I—would miss you very much, Miss Smith,' he said gruffly, adding hastily: 'And so, of course, would Lalage. But I beg you, be on your guard against any further incidents of this nature—and tell me of anything, however

143

trivial it may seem, that disturbs you. Will you promise me this?'

'I promise, sir,' said Hannah, and something, some sort of current, seemed to pass between them. He was just about to speak again when Lallie came bursting into the room, then recollected that she was in the presence of an invalid, and began to tiptoe exaggeratedly towards the settee, saying in sepulchral tones: 'I'm sorry, I forgot you were ill.'

Hannah could not help laughing.

'I am not ill, Lallie dear, just a little shaken up, with a rickety ankle, and a bump on the head. Come along, sit down beside me, and we will play a game if you wish, or you can sketch me.'

'Yes—I'll get my sketching-pad. Then you can sit very quietly while I draw you, and you won't be upset.' Lallie turned at the door. 'But—you really will be well enough for the Grand Dinner Party tomorrow night, won't you, Miss Smith?'

'I'm sure I shall,' Hannah smiled.

'You hadn't forgotten, had you, Papa?' Lallie asked anxiously, and Mr Armstrong shook his head.

'Indeed not. I am greatly looking forward to the occasion, Lalage. But now, if you will excuse me, ladies—' He gave Hannah a half-bow. 'I can see you have a devoted nurse to wait upon you, so I will leave you. Mrs Jones

144

has instructions to bring your meals in on a tray, so you need not move that ankle today. Perhaps, by tomorrow, it will feel a little better.'

'Thank you, sir,' Hannah replied, and he left the room, giving her the impression that he had been about to say something significant when Lallie entered. As she sat and the girl sketched her, she wondered just what he had been about to say. She wished very much that he had said it.

EIGHT

As the morning progressed and Hannah sat quietly, while Lallie's head was bent over the sketch-pad, Hannah thought hard about the momentous events that had occurred since the previous day, and came to some disturbing conclusions. First of all, there was Owen and his unexpected proposal—reinforced by his physical love-making that morning.

She had already thought a great deal about his proposal before being summoned from her room, and the scene in her bedroom that morning had convinced her that she could not really be in love with Owen—not in the sense that she wanted to marry him. Her weakness, as Mr Armstrong had pointed out, had made her vulnerable to his caresses, but still the

145

spark was missing, the spark of wild passion that she would want to feel for a husband. It was only in her dream of the impossible embrace in the firelight that she had felt some of the urgency and the heart-rending tenderness she thought she would like a husband to arouse in her.

No, Owen could be a friend—a good friend, for all that he had become carried away by his feelings that morning—but she could never marry him. She was fond of him, and intended to carry on seeing him even though Mr Armstrong had forbidden him the house, but she could not settle for second-best when it came to deciding her whole future. And she knew in her heart that, much as she admired and liked Owen, he could never be the one man who would come first with her. Love was not something that could be switched on and off at will.

Thinking of Owen's behaviour that morning led Hannah along further trains of thought. Mr Armstrong had been aghast—and quite rightly so. She blushed anew with shame when she thought what he must have seen as he came into the room. But he had generously absolved her from blame—he had been gentle and concerned—he had laid the responsibility for the incident at Owen's door. And there had been that moment when he had looked at her, as he asked whether she wanted to leave—and in spite of herself, she had found herself promising to stay. If only Lallie had not interrupted their conversation! Perhaps Mr Armstrong might have been going to go into more personal matters, and speak as his image had spoken in her dream. Certainly there had been something—some electric spark—between them, and Hannah found her lips curving into a smile as she thought of his care and concern and the feeling of security she had experienced twice within the space of a few hours in his arms, being carried to and from her room.

He had also appeared extremely anxious about her accident, and she could not doubt, from his words, that he wanted to know immediately of anything further that distressed her. Yet, though her emotions told her he cared for her safety and her happiness, a chill seemed to creep up Hannah's spine when she reviewed the events of the night. For who could the mysterious figure in the dark have been? Hannah mentally went through the members of the household. It had not been Lallie—she was too small. It had not been Nanny—she was too clumsy and slow in her movements, and heavy on her feet. It had not been Mr Armstrong, that was certain, for he could never have disguised himself as a woman convincingly. But had Lallie, or Nanny, or even Mr Armstrong himself, persuaded one of the servants to play the part of Caroline?

Hannah could not imagine Lallie doing such

a thing, and the girl's distress at her accident appeared very real. Nanny might have been responsible for the incident, but why, Hannah asked herself helplessly? And she could not even trust Mr Armstrong. As head of the house, he would have more authority than anyone to persuade some maid or kitchen girl to masquerade as his wife.

Hannah's thoughts went round until her head began to ache. What could the purpose be behind such an attack? Who hated her so much—or was insane? Unwillingly, she recalled Mr Armstrong's abrupt changes of mood, and her earlier suspicions that perhaps his wife's death had twisted his brain. He was the only person she could think of in the house who behaved so erratically—and she herself had confided her suspicions to Owen that he might be mad. And now she had told him of the other odd events that had occurred, and was, possibly, playing into his hands if he had some insane plan to kill her.

Abruptly, Hannah pulled herself together. This whole situation was quite ridiculous! She was not in some remote castle in a romantic novelette, with villains stalking the corridors. She was in a family household, in quite an ordinary Welsh village, and it was not a hundred years ago, but the very modern beginning of the Twentieth Century. Such things simply did not happen.

And yet, they had. She knew that if she was

sober and sensible about the affair, she should pack her bags and leave immediately, before some further harm befell her. Once in the hustle and bustle of London, or back with her family, she would be able to think of the events that had occurred since she had arrived at Bethel House as a dream, and nothing more. Yet—perversely, she did not want to leave.

There was Lallie, she told herself, who was beginning to trust her and reveal an affectionate and lovable nature. She could not let Lallie down—and she could not seriously suspect that Lallie wished her harm. A few frights, perhaps, when she had arrived, but nothing like injury or death. She believed that Lallie had found someone she could rely on and trust for the first time in her life, and that if she left, the child would be deeply hurt.

And then there was Mr Armstrong. Hannah's emotions were far more complex concerning her employer.

She could not altogether accept that he was not behind the mysterious incidents that had occurred, and she did not understand his private feelings and thoughts. She did not know how his mind worked—he varied so in his reactions, being unexpectedly gentle at one moment, and harsh the next. But now that he had begun to let down his defences a little as far as his daughter went, Hannah felt it her duty to stay and encourage the process, so that the estrangement between Lallie and her Papa would fade forever, and they would discover a happy father-and-daughter relationship.

She would not admit to herself that there was more—that she was half-frightened, half-fascinated by Gervaise Armstrong, that she listened for his footsteps, and that the room seemed to spring to life when he entered. That her dream, where he had held her in his arms and kissed her, haunted her and filled her with vague longings. He was her employer, no more, she told herself firmly. And he might be insane—she could not even be certain of his sanity.

She set her lips. Yes, she would stay—but from now on, anything—anything at all— that happened to her would be reported immediately to the whole household, and she would demand an explanation. It was a pity there were no locks on the bedrooms doors, but she would put a chair beneath the handle, and refuse to open her door to anyone at all in the night. That, and the fact that she would be on her guard, should ensure her safety.

*   *   *

She spent the day resting, and was carried back up to her room at an early hour by Mr Armstrong, who declared she needed extra sleep after her fright the previous night. Lallie said she would go to bed too, since she wanted to be fresh for her father's birthday the following day. The girl was full of excitement about the Grand Dinner Party, which Hannah had arranged with the cook, as she lay on the settee, discussing the menu. All was prepared, and Lallie complained that she did not know how she would get through the day until the great moment should arrive when they would all don their finery and sit at the huge table in the dining-room, with the candles flickering on the extravagant food.

'I'm afraid I shall have to take things easy, Lallie dear. My ankle is still not very strong,' Hannah said, and Lallie was immediately full of concern.

'But you will be able to walk about—enough to put on your fine gown, won't you, Miss Smith?'

'Oh, yes, I think I shall be able to manage that. But perhaps you would like to go fishing or something tomorrow while I read. Nanny will come and keep an eye on you, I'm sure,' Hannah suggested, smiling, and Nanny said obstinately:

'The river runs deep here, miss. It's not safe for her to fish, is it, my lambie?'

'Oh, Nanny! I'm not going to fall in,' protested Lallie, pulling a face. 'Anyway, if I do, you can always call Mr Jones or Papa. I'm sure Papa would rescue me.'

'There's pools and currents,' said Nanny, giving Hannah a baleful glance, and Hannah could not help wondering exactly what she had done to cause Nanny's ill-will towards any suggestion she herself made. Except that, of course, Nanny was old and set in her ways, and liked to take things easily, spending most of her days on the settee in the drawing-room. The thought sprang to Hannah's mind that perhaps Nanny—after all, she was an unknown quality—perhaps Nanny's senility hid an instability of mind that no-one had ever suspected. Perhaps it was Nanny who was slightly crazy, and who had taken a dislike to Hannah for some fancied slight.

'Well, we'll see. I'm sure there'll be something for you to do, dear,' Hannah said, as she bade Lallie goodnight, and after they had all left her room, she hobbled over to place a chair beneath the handle of her door, before she went to bed. Nothing happened during the night, however, and she awoke the next morning—the morning of Mr Armstrong's birthday—feeling very much recovered.

It had apparently not been the custom for Lallie to give her father a present on his birthday, the day was treated like any other, and apart from offering him good wishes at breakfast, no mention was made of any special celebrations that were to take place until the Dinner Party. He enquired after Hannah's health, then disappeared into his study as usual, leaving Hannah to suggest to Lallie that as the day was so fine, the girl might like to commence her sketch of the house, Hannah's ankle being so much better that, with the aid of a stick, she was able to walk slowly to the bridge where Lallie intended to do her drawing. Hannah seated herself on a chair that Mr Jones brought, and sat enjoying the fresh air and the warm sunlight, the gurgling of the river and the glints of gold on its flowing water, while Lallie perched on the parapet of the bridge and engrossed herself in her drawing.

Hannah dozed, and the day passed pleasantly, but Lallie was full of anticipation for the Grand Party in the evening, and they spent a pleasant hour or so in the afternoon deciding what to wear for the big occasion. Hannah spread out her clothes for the girl's inspection, and Lallie selected a blouse of white silk, heavily trimmed with bunches and frills of finest lace, with a low V-shaped neck, and sheer chiffon sleeves.

'You must wear this,' she declared, and picked out a white chiffon skirt with its rustling taffeta petticoats, and a wide white sash, to accompany the blouse. 'And your pearls, Miss Smith. And do up your hair with this pearl ornament with a white feather. Then you will almost look as though you are going to appear before the King himself.'

Since that was Hannah's most extravagant evening outfit, she was quite satisfied with Lallie's choice, and left the skirt and blouse draped on her bed, ready to change later.

153

Then they went on to consider Lallie's clothes.

'Let's both wear white,' Hannah suggested, as Lallie fumbled in her closet. 'And I will put your hair up the same way as mine, and we'll both flatter your Papa by looking like Duchesses. White is the most fashionable colour of the moment. Look—what about this dress?' And she held up a party frock of white frills, with a pale amber sash. 'The sash matches your eyes, Lallie dear, and I will lend you my topaz aigrette for your hair.'

'Yes, we shall look just like twins,' Lallie agreed enthusiastically. 'Will you really do up my hair, Miss Smith? Nanny always says I'm too young to have it up. She treats me like a baby.'

'Tonight, you shall be a young lady, and your Papa will be proud of you,' promised Hannah, and Lallie clapped her hands. 'Come—let's practise a style that will go with your dress. Sit down before the mirror, and I'll experiment with your hair.'

It was delightful to enjoy a real feminine flutter with ribbons and feathers, combs and hair-pins, and some of their excitement penetrated the rest of the house. Tonight was going to be a big occasion and Hannah was determined that Lallie should enjoy it as much as her father—hopefully—would.

Lallie had made out the place names and written out copies of the menu, and Hannah had already seen to the flowers before they went up to choose their dresses. She was determined that this should be one birthday that Mr Armstrong would never forget.

*　　　*　　　*

And at last, it was time to dress. Hot water was brought up by the maids, and Hannah went into her room after helping Lallie into her white frock and doing up her hair, leaving the girl excitedly preening herself like a bird of paradise in front of the mirror. Twilight was stealing over the countryside, and Hannah pulled her curtains and lit her lamp before she turned to make her own preparations.

She glanced at her dress, spread out on the bed, and a gasp of horror escaped her. Unbelievingly, she touched the fine lace and chiffon and lawn, and with trembling fingers lifted the silk a few inches from the bed. She could not believe her eyes. The lovely white blouse and its matching skirt had been torn to shreds by vicious slashes, and was utterly ruined. It could not possibly be mended, and she would never be able to wear it again.

Then anger flared through her. So this was another piece of work by her mysterious enemy. Well, she decided, shaking with fury, Mr Armstrong should know at once, and the culprit would be found, if they had to question every single person in the house. Hannah told herself that she had taken just about enough, and would have no more nonsense. Her head in the air, two angry spots of colour in her cheeks, she marched from the room and down the corridor, to be halted by the figure of Mr Armstrong coming up from the gallery. He was magnificent in evening dress, but his face was furious.

Hannah opened her mouth to speak, but was checked by Mr Armstrong exclaiming in an outraged manner: 'Lalage! Lalage! Come here at once!'

Lallie appeared from her room, apprehension in every line of her small figure, dressed so daintily for the party.

'Have you been playing tricks on me, or is this some sort of surprise? I don't find it amusing,' said Mr Armstrong, and Lallie flushed.

'Do—do you mean my hair, Papa—?'

'No, I do not. I refer to the fact that my gold cufflinks are missing—one of my most treasured possessions—the last gift that Caroline gave me before she died,' her father fumed. 'Have you taken them from my room? Well? Say something, girl.'

Lallie's eyes began to swim with tears.

'Oh, Papa, no, I—I would never dream of going into your room, or touching your things,' she protested, and Hannah came forward and put her arm protectively about the frail shoulders.

'You cannot seriously suspect Lallie

156

of stealing your valuables, sir?' she said, outraged.

His dark gaze was switched to her face, and she saw that his eyes were blazing.

'Oh? Can you suggest who else might be responsible, Miss Smith? Nanny, for instance? Or Mrs Jones, perhaps?'

'I am certain it was not Lallie,' Hannah countered, and took a deep breath.

'If some valuable objects have been stolen, sir, there is only one thing to be done before calling the authorities. Every person in the house must be searched, and have their room searched, in an effort to find your cuff-links. Perhaps you would like to begin with mine?'

'I will take you at your word, Miss Smith,' he said grimly, and strode past her into her room. He gazed round, inspected the top of the dressing-table, and Hannah pulled her glove drawer open for him to look inside it. To her utter amazement, the lamp caught the gleam of gold. With no attempt at concealment, the gold cuff-links lay on the top of her neat pile of gloves.

Mr Armstrong's mouth twisted as he reached slowly out and picked them up. He turned.

'So you are a thief as well as a slut, Miss Smith,' he said in a low voice, and Hannah gasped. Her head went up.

'You have no right to speak to me like that, sir. I swear I did not touch your cuff-

157

links. This is another of those malicious tricks I mentioned to you before. And you are not the only person on whom one has been played tonight. Look at the state of my gown!' She flung the shreds of white silk and lace in a heap at his feet. 'I was just on my way to tell you that my gown had been slashed to pieces when you came along the corridor.'

'I wish I could believe you—but I cannot forget what I saw here in this very room between you and that—that man! And if you did not touch my cufflinks, how did they manage to find their way into your drawer? I think you owe me some explanations, Miss Smith. Nothing like this ever happened before you came here—people falling down the stairs—midnight masquerades—jewellery disappearing—faces at windows—There has been nothing but trouble here since you arrived,' Mr Armstrong shouted at her, and Hannah turned to the trembling Lallie, who had followed her in, and to Nanny who, roused by the noise, had also come along the corridor.

'Kindly take Lallie downstairs, Nanny,' she said coolly, and Nanny hustled the silent girl from the room. When the door had closed behind them, Hannah let her own anger burst forth.

'You say I need to give you explanations, Mr Armstrong. Well, you most certainly owe some to me! Nothing like this has ever happened before I came, you say—and yet, all of Lallie's other governesses would not stay because of her childish pranks. But I am used to dealing with childish pranks, and I have managed to break through Lallie's distrust. But the things going on in this house are no longer childish pranks—and I might inform you that nothing like this has ever happened to me at any other establishment at which I have been employed.'

She took a deep breath, and continued, while he glared at her: 'Moreover, you are extremely quick to make sure that other people cater to your moods, but what you do not realize is that other people—even governesses—have their feelings too. How do you think I feel when, after I have been pushed down the stairs, and am being offered some sort of physical comfort by a man who loves me—but who has let his emotions carry him away—I am called a slut? I am not a slut, Mr Armstrong! I would have stopped him within a few moments more, had you not entered the room when you did.'

'I saw what I saw,' he grated back, and Hannah flashed:

'You should at least have had the decency to knock. But no—you are the master of the house, you come and go where and when you please, no-one, nothing is sacred to you, not even another's privacy. And now you are accusing me of being a thief! I have told you that someone here has a grudge against me, and it is obvious to me that your cuff-links

159

were appropriated and placed deliberately in my room. Do you suppose, if I had really stolen them, I would have left them lying where all could see? That I would have offered to let you search my room? And how do you think I feel? You at least have your jewels back—but my gown has been ruined—slashed to ribbons. My best evening gown—maliciously destroyed. You have no thought that I might be feeling upset too, have you?'

'It occurs to me, Miss Smith, that you are a young lady who likes attention,' blazed Mr Armstrong, as they faced each other like duellists. 'And no-one can deny that you have had a good deal of attention—becoming locked in the Mirror Room—falling down the stairs—disturbing all our settled routine. How do I know that these stories of yours about someone with a grudge against you are not all inventions of your very fertile mind in order to draw attention to yourself? If you had decided to take my cuff-links, what better way of diverting suspicion from yourself than to slash your own dress to pieces and claim it had been done by another?'

'Are you daring to suggest that I have not been telling you the truth?' gasped Hannah furiously. 'That I am a liar also?'

'Well, you must admit, Miss Smith, that a very good case could be built-up against you,' he answered coolly, and Hannah stood, her knees trembling beneath her, suddenly wanting to laugh hysterically at the irony of it. Here she was, half-suspecting Mr Armstrong of being responsible for the strange events that had happened to her, while he, in his turn, was equally suspicious of her.

'In that case, sir, there is but one course open to me,' she said, coldly and angrily. 'I will pack my bags immediately and leave. I cannot stay in a house where such—such incredible accusations have been made against me.'

'I have made no accusations,' he returned quickly. 'I have merely stated the facts.'

'Nevertheless, I will not be held under unjust suspicion of being a thief—an attention-seeker—a liar,' Hannah flung at him. 'Kindly accept my resignation, sir. I will be gone in half-an-hour.'

'No—no! You shall not go. You must not,' he cried, seizing her wrist, and she tried in vain to twist it away.

'I say I will, sir. You cannot compel me to stay.'

'I order you to stay,' he blazed.

'And I defy you, sir!' she cried furiously. 'Let me go this instant.'

'No. I will not let you go. Not until I have your promise that you will not leave,' he said explosively, and they stood glaring at each other, while he held her wrist in a tight grasp.

'Tomorrow I must go to see one of my tenant farmers some distance away. I refuse to come back and find you gone,' he stated, after

161

a moment.

'Your business is no longer my concern, sir. I have resigned from your employ,' Hannah threw back. 'Kindly be so good as to leave me to pack.'

'I will not accept your resignation, Miss Smith. Not until these—these disturbing matters have been sorted out to my satisfaction,' he told her, but he let her wrist go, and Hannah rubbed it with her other hand, for his grip had been painfully tight.

'I have not said I disbelieve you—but you must admit the strangeness of your claims,' he went on, more reasonably. 'Why should such events be sparked off by your presence here? I need time to think—to consider—to enquire into the circumstances. Besides, there is no train at this time of the night. And Lalage— would you desert her?'

Hannah was silent. The thought of Lallie sitting bewilderedly downstairs in her party dress, all her pleasure in the Grand Dinner spoiled, touched her heart.

'I will stay, sir,' she said slowly, 'but only on one condition. I wish a full enquiry to be made into the events I have reported to you. Not until I am satisfied that the culprit has been exposed will I be happy to remain here. Otherwise, I will stay with Lallie, but with your permission, we will return to your London home.'

'And—when I come back tomorrow

evening? You will be here?' he demanded, and she nodded.

He sighed, as though he had won a victory.

'Very well then, Miss Smith. And then, I promise you, my work shall be put entirely on one side until you and I have sorted out exactly what is happening in this house. I am afraid I lost my temper. I apologize. I do not, of course, suspect for a moment that you are responsible for the disturbances that have beset us—nor do I think you took my cuff-links. It was just the sudden shock of seeing them in your drawer—I am just as baffled as you must be yourself.'

Hannah accepted his apology with a small inclination of her head.

'I am afraid your Dinner Party has been ruined, and Lallie will be very disappointed. She was so looking forward to pleasing you, and dressing up for the occasion,' she said regretfully, and he turned away, pushing his cuff-links into position.

'Lalage is already dressed—so is Nanny—and so am I. If you can find a suitable gown to replace the one that was slashed, Miss Smith, the Dinner Party will continue as planned,' he declared grimly. 'What has just happened is between us two—Lalage and Nanny need know no more than that the missing cuff-links have been found. I—do not wish to disappoint them. Lalage is already upset at your accident.'

'That is very thoughtful of you, sir,'

said Hannah, surprised at his concern for his daughter. 'If you will give me a few moments—I will try to hurry—'

'And I will go down to ease the situation and inform the cook that the Dinner Party will be commencing shortly,' he said, and paused in the doorway.

'Don't worry too much about your gown, Miss Smith. You always look beautiful, whatever you are wearing,' he said, so quickly that Hannah was not certain she had heard him correctly, but a glow went through her all the same at his words, and she hurried into another evening outfit of pale primrose, and pulled her hair into a knot on her neck, since there was no time to put it up properly. She pinned a yellow silk rose to her bosom, pulled on her matching gloves, and went down.

To her surprise, she heard the sound of Lallie's laugh as she reached the drawing-room door, and when she went inside, it was to find Mr Armstrong pouring outrageous flattery on his daughter, begging Nanny to introduce him to the 'beautiful young lady in white'. Hannah's heart warmed. He was obviously determined that the disastrous events of the evening should not spoil Lallie's pleasure, and she flung herself into the charade with him, formally presenting him to his hostess, Miss Lalage Armstrong, while Lallie blushed and bubbled with laughter.

They sat down to dinner, and although

the upsetting scene that had just taken place meant that neither Hannah nor Mr Armstrong ate very much of what was placed before them, Lallie bloomed, as each dish was formally carried in—the soup, the fish, the roast beef, the venison—and Mr Armstrong declared as he tucked into the food:

'I swear, ma'am, I have seen you before, but you are looking so delightful tonight that I hardly recognize you.'

'Oh, Papa!' Lallie giggled, and added, with a quaint assumption of formal manners: 'I believe I have seen you, too, sir. But tonight you seem—well, different.'

'That is because I have fallen beneath the spell of your entrancing eyes, my dear Miss Armstrong,' her father teased, and only Hannah noticed the lines of strain about his mouth as he romped with Lallie, making certain that she had as pleasant an evening as he could.

After the meal, Hannah announced: 'And now, it is time for the dancing, ladies and gentlemen. Mr Jones has kindly consented to play upon his fiddle. Show him in, Lallie dear.'

Mr Jones, in his best Sunday suit, came in carrying his instrument, and since Nanny said, as she wheezed her way onto the settee, that she could not dance, she was too old for such things, and Hannah's ankle was still painful, Mr Armstrong and Lallie romped round the room to the strains of Mr Jones' fiddle, until

Mr Armstrong declared he was exhausted.

Mr Jones, highly entertained by the fun, disappeared, and Mr Armstrong said to Lallie:

'A glass of wine, my dear young lady, before you retire?'

They all sat round sipping the champagne Hannah had ordered for the occasion, and Lallie said sleepily: 'Have you enjoyed yourself, Papa? Has this been a birthday you will never forget? That's what Miss Smith and I planned.'

Mr Armstrong's eyes flickered to Hannah, then back to his daughter.

'Yes, Lallie,' he said quietly, using her pet name for the first time. 'This has indeed been an evening I will never forget.'

'I'm glad,' Lallie said drowsily, almost asleep over her champagne, and she took her father's hand and leaned against his shoulder without hesitation. Hannah's heart throbbed as she saw him pat the small hand, and put an arm round the frail shoulders. At last, the barriers were down between Gervaise Armstrong and his daughter. At least this evening had achieved something—something very important—she told herself, and it seemed the most natural thing in the world that Mr Armstrong should sweep up the girl in his arms and carry her up the stairs to her room, and kiss her goodnight, before Hannah helped her off with her finery, brushed out her thick brown hair, and settled her in bed.

'You know something, Miss Smith?' Lallie said, before she drifted asleep. 'I feel different now I know Papa really loves me. I don't feel as though I want to be naughty any more, I want to please him. Because I love him too, you know—I really do—I always wanted him to be a person I could love, and now I have a real Papa who cares about me. He called me 'Lallie', did you hear—?'

And her eyes closed contentedly.

NINE

The following morning, Hannah awoke to find that the spell of fine weather appeared to be breaking. The sky was dull, and a sort of yellow light indicated the approach of a possible summer storm. However, within the house, as they breakfasted, there was a new and happy communication between Mr Armstrong and his daughter, for Lallie had now attained complete trust in her father, and she spoke and laughed with him without fear or hesitation.

Hannah was glad to see that he responded, and, though he was rather quiet, he made every effort to show Lallie that her affection was reciprocated.

When she heard that he was obliged to go and see his tenant farmer, Lallie's face clouded, and she begged to be allowed to come too but, on this point, her father was gently insistent.

'No, my dear, I'm afraid not. But I shall be back tonight, and in the meantime, you have Miss Smith. I cannot be with you all the time, you know; you must get used to the fact that I have business to see to, and other things to occupy me from time to time.'

'Yes, I suppose so,' Lallie responded, but when Mr Armstrong was preparing to depart, just after breakfast, she clung to him, and lifted her face to be kissed.

'Hurry home, Papa,' she said, reluctantly letting him go, and he smiled—a smile that Hannah would not have believed possible when she had first met him—and tilted up his daughter's chin.

'I shall, and I'll be back in no time, Lallie, you'll see. Now, wave me off like a good girl.'

Lallie stood beside Hannah, and the two of them waved as the carriage turned out of the drive and clattered across the bridge over the river. Mr Armstrong waved his hat out of the window, until a turn in the lane hid the carriage from view, and he was gone.

'Oh, well! Now what are we going to do? I think I shall work on my Country Notebook. I mean to present it to Papa when it's finished,' Lallie confided, as they turned to go in through the front door. 'Do you think he will be pleased?'

'I think he'll be delighted, darling,' Hannah

told her. She stood for a moment looking at the sky. 'What an odd colour those clouds are. I fear your Papa may run into some rain on this trip, and we may have a real storm. The wind is getting up, too.'

'Shall you be going to church again, Miss Smith?' Lallie enquired, and Hannah shook her head. She had already made her plans for the day. Mr Jones could not take her to church in the trap, as he was driving Mr Armstrong, and she could not walk as far as the village, for her ankle was still not completely healed. In any case, she had other things to do, and although she regretted that she would not see Owen or Mrs Richards, it was far more important for the mysterious events of last night and the past weeks to be investigated. Hannah had come to the conclusion that Lallie and Nanny—as well as Mr Armstrong—could not have been responsible for her accident and the stolen cuff-links and her slashed gown, and that left only the employees of the house. She meant to find out more about them while Mr Armstrong was away and, if possible, confront him with the culprit when he returned.

She had to admit that she did not know exactly how to go about her task, but she began by making her way to the kitchen and servants' quarters, words forming themselves in her head.

When she appeared in the huge, old, country kitchen, where food was simmering and baking and roasting, all the maids and the cook and Mrs Jones turned, and a hush fell over their chatter.

'Good morning,' said Hannah, pleasantly. 'I'm so sorry to trouble you, Mrs Jones, but Mr Armstrong has asked me to have a look at the rooms where the maids, and all who live-in, are lodged. He is thinking of having some alterations made, and apparently these rooms are included in his plans.'

She paused, and the servants exchanged glances, obviously baffled. Hannah hoped they would accept her completely untrue statement without question.

'Naturally,' she continued, with a smile, 'I cannot intrude on your privacy, but I wonder if you could each show me your own room—only for a brief inspection, you understand. That is, of course, if you are not too busy.'

'No, we'll be glad to oblige, miss,' Mrs Jones said at once, and during the next few hours before luncheon, all the maids and kitchen girls—even the cook—took Hannah on an inspection of their rooms.

She found their quarters clean and neat, mostly with few personal possessions scattered about, since when the family departed for London again, the girls—even cook—would no longer be required, and would go back to their homes, leaving only Mr and Mrs Jones to oversee the mansion.

Hannah took a notebook with her, and

pretended to note down details of space, and so on, but she was actually looking for some clue that would give away the identity of her mysterious assailant. She found nothing suspicious, however and, at last, Mrs Jones took her up to the rooms that she and Mr Jones occupied, which were naturally furnished with their own treasures, since they lived in the house permanently, and showed her round. Hannah was frustrated and baffled. She had some across nothing—nothing to give her any idea to work on.

'Of course, not everyone lives in' Mrs Jones told her, as they descended the back-stairs again. 'A few of the servants come in daily, as you know, miss, since they live quite near. But Mr Armstrong has always seemed satisfied with this arrangement before.'

'Oh, no, it's nothing to do with your running of the staff, Mrs Jones. Purely a matter of—er—facilities provided for the maids, and so on,' Hannah invented glibly. 'You must admit that the house could do with a little modernization.'

Mrs Jones nodded her agreement, and proceeded to tell Hannah a long tale that involved someone becoming shut in a cupboard and being unable to make anyone hear her, and Hannah lingered, watching the servants as they moved past her, going about their duties. None of them seemed the least bit out of the ordinary. Her plan had come to nothing.

Then she stiffened, and turned, as a door near them opened, and a woman dressed in outdoor clothes came in. Dark hair neatly pulled back beneath her plain hat, a long dark coat. Eyes cast down, she bobbed a curtsey to Mrs Jones and Hannah, then brushed through the small back hall into the kitchen.

'Who—who was that?' Hannah asked casually, trying not to reveal her inner turmoil. For the woman had brought with her the unmistakable fragrance of lily-of-the-valley—and Hannah suddenly recollected something that had previously slipped her mind—that the figure at the top of the stairs had also smelled of that same fresh, clean scent.

'That's Megan—Mrs Evans, miss. She lives out,' Mrs Jones responded willingly, and leaned forward, only too pleased to gossip. 'A strange woman she is, indeed, and I wouldn't hire her if it wasn't that she has such a good hand with the pastry. But she keeps herself very much to herself, and she and Mair belong to the Reverent Joseph's funny religion, not good chapel, like the rest of us. Something about being Brothers and Sisters in the Blood of the Lamb. Course, they do no harm, but— well, there's something about Megan—and Mair—always been a bit odd, they have, since they were converted to the Reverend Joseph. Quiet, like, and—well, just odd, somehow,' she finished.

Hannah's heart was pounding.

'You mean—Megan is Mair's mother?' she enquired.

'Yes, and a real nuisance Mair is, hanging about house when it's empty. You never know where you'll find her. She treats the place like her own—you'd swear she lived here, not in their cottage down the lane,' Mrs Jones said indignantly, adding in a low tone: 'But I'm sorry for the girl, somehow, having no Dada, like. Bryn Evans was killed, you know, an accident on the farm. Tragic, it was. You'd think Megan would marry again, there's plenty would have her, but she doesn't seem to want them. So there's just her and Mair.'

'I—er—I haven't seen Mair about lately,' Hannah commented, her face averted, and Mrs Jones shrugged.

'Oh, that one! She's seen when she wants to be seen—goes her own way, does Mair. But since she got told off for talking to Miss Lallie, I haven't seen her about much either. And real glad I am too. She won't help in the house at all. Nothing but trouble, that girl.'

'I see. Well, thank you, Mrs Jones,' Hannah said, with a warm smile, and she made her way back to the front of the house, where she sat down at the writing desk in one of the little parlours, her mind racing.

She mustn't be too hasty—she mustn't jump to conclusions—yet she knew she was right! It all fitted! Things came vaguely back to her—

173

Lallie talking about herself and Mair being blood sisters—making a blood pact. Probably Mair had tried to initiate the young daughter of the house into her own strange religion, whatever it was. And not only that, she regarded the house as her own, Mrs Jones had said, wandering round alone when the rooms were shut-up and empty and the family away.

And then Hannah had come along, and forbidden her to see Lallie again, pointing out Mair's more humble position, and making it clear that she would not tolerate Mair's friendship with Lallie—even, Hannah recalled, threatening that Mair's mother would be dismissed. And if there was no man in the home and they needed the money her mother earned—

No wonder Mair should hold a grudge against her. And, with the bitter and vengeful nature that Hannah suspected the girl possessed, no wonder she had begun to try and get her own back on the governess who had over-ruled her authority with Lallie. Hannah shuddered suddenly, as a cold chill went up her spine. Probably Megan Evans had no notion of her daughter's activities, finding solace in her religion for her widowhood. She would not know if Mair stole her perfume, slipped out of their cottage at nights to wander the house and play ghost in order to frighten Hannah.

For Hannah had no doubt now that Mair—that girl whom she herself had sensed was evil—was the culprit behind all the strange occurrences that had happened. Even the candles going out by themselves on the night they arrived—probably Lallie, who had then been only too willing to give her new governess a fright, had a standing arrangement with Mair that every new governess should receive the same treatment when the family came to Bethel House. For at the time, she had regarded Mair as her only friend, until Hannah had won her confidence, and her father had begun to take an interest in her doings.

It had been Lallie who had locked Hannah in the Mirror Room, too, and tapped on her window that first night, but Hannah had no doubt that the rest of the odd happenings— Caroline's face, the doll with the pin through its heart, her accident on the stairs—and the catastrophes of the previous evening—had all been Mair's doing, and hers alone.

The more she thought about it, the more she became convinced that she was right, and she could hardly wait for Mr Armstrong to return home so that she could tell him what she had discovered, and he could question the girl. It was no use trying to question her herself, Hannah thought, since Mair would simply deny everything, but if the master of the house were to instigate a thorough investigation, Mair would probably be frightened into confessing. Hannah went over to the window, and looked out at the dismal sky and the trees tossing in the wind. Oh, hurry, hurry home, she said in her mind to her employer! And something made her add: 'Before something else happens'.

*   *   *

All the rest of that day, Hannah was uneasy. She had sought for someone who hated her—or someone who was mad; and in Mair, she suspected she had found both, although probably the girl had not yet gone completely over the edge into absolute insanity. But there was no denying that she was evil, and Hannah half-expected a wild figure to leap out at her from behind a curtain, or from a doorway, with a knife at the ready.

Her sole means of safety lay, she knew, in the fact that Mair did not know she had been discovered, and thought she was still unsuspected. But if she were to find out that Hannah knew she was the culprit—and Mr Armstrong was out of the house—Hannah shuddered to think what action she might take to silence the only person who knew of her identity.

So the day wore on, and Hannah tried to be with Lallie and Nanny as much as possible, while all of them seemed to be on edge, the threatening storm giving Nanny a headache and making Lallie petulant. She was waiting eagerly for her father, but he had still not returned when her bed-time came, though as she was drinking her hot milk, a sudden growl of thunder in the distance, and a pattering of raindrops on the window glass announced that the storm was approaching.

'I do hope Papa isn't caught in it,' Lallie fretted, and Hannah tried to soothe her.

'I expect he'll be home soon, dear. If I were you, I should try and go to sleep as fast as possible, so you're all ready to be bright and cheerful for him in the morning.'

'Yes, I will,' Lallie agreed. She turned to Hannah, 'Are you afraid of storms, Miss Smith?'

'Not really. They clear the air, and everything's all fresh and clean afterwards. No, I can't say that a storm bothers me very much,' Hannah said, deliberately casual. 'Why, dear? Storms don't frighten you, do they?'

'Well—only a little bit,' Lallie said reluctantly. She added, as she went up to bed, and Hannah accompanied her, not wanting to leave her to go up on her own with the thunder rumbling in the distance: 'But if I come into your room—that's only if the storm's a really bad one—that will be all right, won't it? You won't mind?'

'Of course I won't. But I expect you'll be fast asleep by then, and you won't hear a thing. And in the morning, your Papa will be back,' Hannah said cheerfully, as she helped Lallie prepare for bed, and then tucked her in under the covers. The velvet curtains shut out the strange murky gloom that was over the countryside, and muffled the sound of the heavy raindrops, which were still only spattering now and then.

'In any case, the storm may move the other way, and miss us altogether. Let's hope so,' Hannah said, bending to kiss Lallie. 'Goodnight now, darling.'

She left the girl settled for slumber, and went down to the drawing-room, where she sat with Nanny for a while, her ears strained for the sound of Mr Armstrong's return. But he was late, and when she eventually decided to retire herself, he had still not come home.

It was not until she came to put the chair beneath the handle of her door that she remembered Lallie's plea that she should be allowed to come to her governess for comfort if the storm woke her, and Hannah, listening to the now-pelting rain, and the heavy gusts of wind that shook the windows in their frames, decided to leave the chair where it was. Mair would surely not attempt anything in this weather, and she still did not know Hannah suspected her. And in the morning, Mr Armstrong would be back and all would be well. Hannah sent up a fervent prayer for his safe return as she slid between the sheets of her bed, and, with the rain beating on her windows, tried to sleep.

To her surprise, she fell asleep almost at

once, and when she woke, it was to a gigantic crack of thunder that seemed to shake the house to its foundation. A few seconds later, there was a violent streak of lightning that flickered even through her closed curtain-cracks, and lit up the room with a lurid light. Hannah started up, her heart beginning to pound in her throat. In the lightning-flash, she had seen that she was not alone in her room. The door stood wide open, and a dark figure was standing silently a few feet from her bed.

'Who's there? Is that you, Lallie?' demanded Hannah, sitting up and lighting the lamp with trembling fingers, while the storm beat about the house. The lamp-light bloomed softly, and in its glow, she saw that the door still stood open, but the silent figure had gone. She thought, though, that she could detect a faint scent on the air of lily-of-the-valley.

Anger and determination replaced Hannah's fear. Mair was up to her tricks again and, this time, she should not get away. Hannah pulled on her green chiffon robe, and slid her feet into her slippers, then picked up the lamp, and crossed to the door. She'd catch Mair—shake a confession from her—have some proof to give to Mr Armstrong in the morning. Resolutely, she went out of the door, and advanced into the corridor.

It was just as she had thought! The dark figure, which looked as though it was wearing some sort of robe, with a hood pulled up over

179

the head, was standing at the far end of the passage, near the turn to the gallery. Even as Hannah watched, and the thunder rolled and rumbled round the house, the hooded figure lifted a hand and beckoned, then turned and disappeared round the bend.

'I know it's you, Mair!' called Hannah, as steadily as she could. 'You're not going to get away with this, you know! Stop—come back this instant!'

She ran to the end of the corridor, the lamplight giving her confidence, and saw that the figure could move just as quickly as she. Now it was standing at the far end of the gallery, where another corridor branched off, and as soon as Hannah appeared, it beckoned once again, and was gone.

Hannah ran on, to find her prey standing now at the same distance away, halfway up a flight of stairs, on a small landing.

'I'm coming no further, Mair. This is ridiculous,' Hannah called, having to raise her voice as the thunder rumbled and drowned her words. The wind was howling furiously and the rain battering the outside walls, but Hannah was unaware of the storm. She had all her attention focussed on the hooded figure which seemed to be playing some macabre game with her, luring her up into the top floors of the house.

Angrily, Hannah ran forward as fast as she could, and mounted the stairs, her gaze fixed on the swiftly-gliding figure before her. If only she could catch Mair! But the figure was too quick for her, and managed to keep always just outside the circle of her lamplight. There was no stopping and beckoning now, however, the episode had turned into a chase, with Hannah determined to catch the girl, and the hooded figure just as determined to evade her.

Mair obviously knew her way about the house very well, and Hannah began to breathe quickly as she ran along corridors, and up flights of stairs until, at last, she judged they must be in the attics of the house. Overhead, the storm seemed very loud, and she could hear the rain on the roof. Then, she turned a corner and found herself in a small bare room with a ladder leading upwards to an opened trap-door, into which the wind howled and the rain was falling in torrents. Quickly she looked round. There was no sign of Mair, and Hannah headed for the stair-ladder and began to climb, while the wind whipped at her robe, and her hair flew about her head, and the lamp went out.

She emerged, panting, to find herself on the roof of the house, and the force of the gale almost knocked her over, so that she tottered and threw her arms round a tall chimney nearby, the lamp falling from her hand and shattering.

'Well, Mair, here I am,' Hannah shouted into the storm. 'Was this what you wanted?'

She waited to see the hooded figure emerge from behind some angle or battlement on the roof, and was shocked when she heard a mocking laugh behind her. Still clutching the chimney, she turned her head. The hooded figure was looking up at her through the trapdoor, she could just make out Mair's features in the darkness that every now and then was cut by a stab of lightning. Then, to Hannah's horror, the face disappeared, the trap slammed shut and she heard, even above the sound of the gale, the grating of a bolt being drawn.

She had been fooled—duped—somehow Mair had hidden herself—possibly even just behind the door as she entered the small bare room, intent on her quarry—and now she was locked out, a prisoner on the roof of the house, with the wind waiting to grasp her and whirl her over the edge to her death below, and the storm gathering force all about her, the rain drenching her to the skin, the thunder menacing her, the lightning making her shut her eyes in horror, for fear it struck the chimney she was clasping so tightly.

And no-one knew where she was! Grimly, Hannah fought back the desire to burst into tears of fright and despair, and clung with all her strength to the chimney, until her arms began to tremble from the effort. She must not let go! Once she allowed the wind to catch her, she would be powerless against the force of the gale.

Hold on! she told herself, her eyes shut fast. He'll come! Somehow, he'll come!

It was odd that, at a moment when she was so near to death, her mind should choose to tell her that she loved Gervaise Armstrong, and had indeed loved him almost since the day she had met him.

And love overcame all things, even evil such as Mair had perpetrated that night. Hannah clung on, with one thought running over and over through her mind. He'll come! He'll come! He'll come!

TEN

The storm seemed to gather itself and burst afresh on Hannah as she clung, shaking and with clenched teeth, to the chimney. Thunder rolled about her, lightning darted wildly, so that she could see the top of the house clearly if she opened her eyes. She was shivering, and the wind, howling like a mad thing, seemed to chill her through her soaking robe and nightdress to her very bones, while her hair streamed in rats' tails round her shoulders.

She realized that it would do no good to call for help. There was no-one to hear, and her voice would be lost in the fury of the elements. She would have to wait until the storm had

183

passed, until the morning had come, until someone was about in the yard or around the house. But she feared she might not be able to last the long night. Her arms were already weak from clinging to the chimney, and she was afraid that her strength would give way and she would be torn and snatched by the gale, thrown over the edge of the parapet, unable to cling to safety any longer.

Perhaps she could try to get herself into a more secure position, she thought, where she would be a little better sheltered from the wind. The top of the house was a mass of jutting angles, chimneys, dormers, and if she could see a corner where she could perhaps sit down, protected from the gale, she might be better able to withstand her ordeal.

In the next lightning-flash, she tried to see where she was in relation to the rest of the house, and discovered that, a little to her left, the battlemented front of the building rose, and there was an angle where two parts of the roof met, with quite a deep dip in between. Hannah crawled down the chimney, tearing her chiffon robe to shreds as she did so, and felt about with her feet, her arms still clasped round the brick structure that represented her security. Her heels and ankles were gashed and bleeding, but one of her feet found the dip and, holding her breath, she waited until the wind seemed to have abated a little, then let herself down into the sheltered hollow.

As she sat there, huddled up with her back against the front battlements of the house, she was able to relax a little, though she lay in a pool of water. So long as she kept her head down, the wind could not stir her from her shelter, and she could let her aching arms and back relax.

She wondered what Mair had hoped would happen to her. Obviously the wind was the danger, and Mair must have expected that she would either be swept off the roof to her death—Hannah felt sick with vertigo when she thought how high up she was—or that exposure for a night to weather like this would make her ill. That danger was yet to be overcome, for there were hours and hours of darkness ahead, and Hannah was already feeling dizzy and sick.

She thought of Gervaise Armstrong with longing, a fierce and furious longing to be safely held in his arms. She hoped she would not die before she could tell him that she loved him—loved him utterly and with all her heart and soul and body. She knew now why she had been unable to commit herself to Owen—it was because deep within her was a passion that had sprung into being during the dream by the fire—a dream that she realized now had not been a dream at all, but had actually happened.

And he—surely such passion could not be one-sided? He loved her too, she knew it, and clung to the thought of his love as she lay and the rain beat down on her unprotected skin. So many things she understood now—his black moods when Owen had come on the scene were the result of jealousy, for he feared she might be falling in love with the young doctor.

But he was the man he was, he could not accept that a second love could enter his life after Caroline—he had been cautious, suspicious, surly even, yet she knew as surely as she knew that the sun would rise tomorrow that he loved her—oh, if God would only spare her for her to tell him that she loved him for his very moodiness—that she would never have found a man to measure up to him—that Owen and his love-making meant nothing to her compared to the flame that swept through her veins when she thought of his arms about her in front of the fire.

Hannah began to imagine she must be becoming slightly delirious.

The storm had lessened slightly, the thunder was rolling off into the distance, and she thought she could hear sounds—voices ... She raised herself carefully on one elbow. Yes! That was the sound of carriage wheels! And Lallie's voice!

'It's Miss Smith, Papa—she's disappeared—'

'Lallie! Lallie!' screamed Hannah, struggling against the wind. The carriage must have come round to the front door below her, and Lallie was waiting inside to speak to her

Papa. If only she could make them hear her.

'Lallie! Gervaise!' she screamed over and over, like a mad woman, but through the howling of the wind, she heard a sound that seemed to her like the lid of a tomb dropping upon her—the closing of the heavy front door. They had gone inside, and Mr Jones would not hear her, for he was occupied with taking the carriage round to the stable yard at the back of the house, far away from the place where Hannah lay.

It was then that Hannah almost gave way to complete despair. Tears of frustration and cold and misery streamed down her face. They would search the house—but no-one would think of looking on the roof. Why should they? Who would imagine that she had gone up to the roof—in the middle of the night, with a storm raging, especially when she had already told Lallie how she hated heights and had refused to inspect the roof in broad daylight?

Hannah shifted her position in the pool of muddy water, full of leaves and debris from the gutters, and laid her face down on her arms, and wept. By the time they found her, it would be too late—if, indeed, they ever found her at all. But then she set her jaw firmly, and tried to check the chattering of her teeth. She must not give in! Someone would go outside—some time. If only she could keep her mind clear, she might be able to attract attention yet. And, giving her strength that pulsed through her, was the knowledge that her beloved employer was home. He was near—he would find her—somehow, he would rescue her, she told herself.

The storm had faded now to a far-off rumbling, but the wind still tore at the house, and the rain still fell. Hannah's eyes had become a little accustomed to the dark, and she tried to make plans. If anyone should open the front door again, she must lean over the battlement as far as she could without being swept away, and call—scream—try to attract attention.

Yet at the very thought of even looking down from her terrible position, she felt again a sick vertigo. She was afraid she might fall, her hands shaking so much now that she would be unable to cling to the stonework, her voice only a croak, the thought of that dreadful sheer drop beneath her drawing her like a magnet.

She could not do it! She could not! And yet, she must. Only if she could attract attention could she be rescued. And even while she battled with herself, her heart leaped as she heard the very sounds she had thought she might never hear. The front door was opening far below, and there was a voice calling into the wind—a dearly loved, familiar voice, deep with anxiety.

'Hannah! Hannah! Darling—where are you? Can you hear me? Hannah! '

Trembling all over, Hannah managed to crawl up the edge of the battlement, and peered over as far as she dared, clinging frantically to the stones. She could see a light—a lantern—far, far down below, but even though she knew he was there, she could not see him, only the light.

'Gervaise! Gervaise! I'm here!' she screamed, as loudly as she could, but the wind tore the words from her lips, and the light moved further on.

'Hannah! Where are you?'

She could hear his voice giving orders to someone, and other lanterns moved, as he sent some of the men off to search the grounds. Hannah tried again, but her voice was not strong enough to reach him.

'I'm here, Gervaise! Look up—I'm on the roof! Gervaise—oh, God, I'm here!' she cried desperately.

He called again, and again, and Hannah, her heart pulsing like a hammer in her throat, leaned further forward in her anxiety, trying to make him hear.

But it was no use, his lantern was moving away, and Hannah felt all hope go with it. She made one last effort, clinging as she leaned over the battlement into the deadly wind—but her hands slipped suddenly on the wet stones, and she thought in that frantic second that the wind, whipping her hair about her face, had her and she was going over the edge. A wild scream tore from her throat, as she grappled and scrabbled for her balance, and the sound reached him at last.

'Hannah! Is that you, darling? For God's sake, tell me where you are!'

Clinging on by her fingertips, Hannah sobbed: 'I'm—on the—roof, Gervaise! Oh, save me! Please save me!'

His lantern was directly below her now.

'Did you say—on the roof, Hannah? Are you on the roof?'

'Yes,' Hannah wept, the light blurring before her eyes. 'I'm falling, Gervaise! I'm falling!'

'No, my love, you're not. Hold on tightly! I won't let you fall,' he called, urgently. 'There! You're not falling now, are you?'

Hannah hid her face against the wet stone, and managed to easy her body back into her safe little pool of mud.

'No, but I'm so afraid. I was trapped on the roof—the trap-door was bolted behind me,' Hannah croaked, stunned by her narrow escape, and his voice came up to her, strong and encouraging.

'Hold on, my love. I'm coming. Hold on tightly. You won't fall. I'm coming now.'

Hannah sank dizzily back into her little corner, her heart pounding, fresh hope surging through her. He was coming! He would find her—rescue her—just as she had known he would. Oh, thank you, God, she found herself murmuring over and over. Dear Lord, thank you!

It seemed an eternity before the trap was flung back, and lights bobbed up onto the roof. Hannah tried to crawl towards them crying with relief, but she was so weak and soaked with gutter debris that she could hardly summon the energy to move from her little corner. But it didn't matter. Figures moved about on the roof, and in answer to her feeble cry of 'Gervaise!' she found herself enfolded, mud, rain, leaves and all, in a fierce embrace, while his lips sought hers passionately, and he held her as though he would never let her go.

'My darling—my darling—are you all right? Oh, Hannah, my dearest love, I was so afraid something had happened to you—that you were hurt—dead—' he said fervently, his hands clasping her body so tightly she thought she would have bruises in the morning. But she was clinging to him with equal passion.

'Gervaise—oh, thank God, my love, my dearest—I wanted you—I prayed for you to come. I was afraid I would die before I could tell you how much I love you,' she babbled wildly, and they clung together in a mutual delirium of newly-discovered emotion while the rain beat down until Gervaise suddenly recollected her plight and lifted his head, reluctantly, from a kiss that Hannah thought would sear her to her very soul.

'Hannah, darling, you're cold as a stone, and

wet-through. We must get you down from this death-trap as soon as we can,' he said gently. 'Can you walk, love? If I hold you?'

'I—think so—I don't know—' gasped Hannah, and seized his arm. 'Be careful of the wind, Gervaise. It will blow you over—'

'No, darling, I have a rope tied round my waist, and the men are holding me. Come—let's get you to warmth and shelter,' he said, and he half-carried, half-dragged the filthy, sodden figure of Hannah to where the lights were waiting.

She was passed carefully down by willing hands, into the small bare room, and then Gervaise took over and, cradling her in his arms, close to his strong chest, he took her down from the attics to a small parlour where a bright fire was burning, and Mrs Jones fussed round, covering Hannah's filthy rags with a thick blanket, and bustling off to oversee the preparation of a hot bath immediately.

Hannah sat, the blanket beginning to warm her, on Gervaise's lap, for he would not let her go, and managed to laugh shakily.

'I don't imagine you ever thought you would declare your love to a creature such as I must look at this moment—black with dirt, my hair soaked, my clothes ripped to shreds—'

'That part I approve of,' he teased, as both of them soared up into a sort of hysterical joy at Hannah's escape from danger, and he thrust his arms beneath the blanket and

192

pushed it away, so that her ragged gown barely concealed her body. He covered her with kisses, and she held his black head against her breast with fierce joy.

'When I saw you—and the doctor—I went mad with jealousy, my darling. I have been mad with jealousy all the time, thinking you loved him,' he said, and Hannah twined her fingers in his hair.

'That night by the fire—I wanted you then—and I have not stopped wanting you ever since, although I did not know it until I thought I was going to die tonight,' she told him. 'It was Mair who did all those foolish things, Gervaise, I was going to tell you tomorrow, but she came to my room tonight disguised in a robe and hood, and I tried to catch her, and she lured me up onto the roof and shut me there. I was so afraid I would never see you again—'

'Hush, love. We will deal with Mair and her dangerous meddling tomorrow—I will make sure she has no chance to try to do to anyone else what she so nearly did to you. Oh, my love—!' His arms closed about her again, pulling her against him so that her bare breasts were crushed and she could feel all the muscles of his body straining to her. Willingly, she responded, exploring him with her hands, until they broke away, and he gave a crooked smile.

'I fear we must wait for what we both desire, my sweet, until we are married. Mrs

193

Jones would be so scandalized if she came in and found us entwined on the rug. Or Lallie. The poor child was so anxious about you—she had gone to your room during the storm, and found you gone—and she roused Nanny and all the servants, and they searched the whole house, from top to bottom,' he told her, wrapping the blanket about her again, and cradling her with her head against his shoulder. 'It was then that I arrived, and when I heard that the house had been searched, I decided you must have been taken outside, or gone outside for some reason. That was why I went out—for if you were not in the house, it was only logical to suppose you were somewhere in the grounds.'

'And you found me! Somehow, I knew you would, it was the thought of your love—and my love for you that kept me going when the storm was raging, and the wind almost tore me from the roof to my death,' murmured Hannah, kissing his neck.

There was a sudden knock at the door, and Lallie's anxious face appeared. When she saw the two of them together by the fire, she rushed forward and threw her arms about them both.

'Oh, Papa! You found her! Are you all right, Miss Smith? I went to your room, and I was so worried when we couldn't find you. I love you, you know,' she confessed, her brown eyes warm with concern as she saw the scratches

194

and bruises on Hannah's face and arms.

'Oh, Lallie darling, I love you too,' exclaimed Hannah, and Mr Armstrong cleared his throat.

'Well, it's a fortunate thing that we all love each other,' he said drily. 'Because from now on, we're going to be a family, Lallie. How do you feel about Miss Smith changing her name and becoming Mrs Armstrong—my wife?'

Lallie's face lit up with delight, then she wrinkled her nose.

'I shan't mind once she's had a bath,' she said, with a dryness that exactly matched her father's, and father and daughter grinned at each other. 'At the moment, though, she's a bit smelly and dirty. But I won't mind once we've cleaned her up a bit.'

'My own sentiments exactly, Lallie,' said Gervaise Armstrong softly. 'We'll each love her and take care of her in our own way.' And he bent his head and kissed Hannah, who was laughing, full on the lips, while Lallie looked on with delighted approval, as though she had engineered the whole thing.

'Papa *and* Mama,' she pronounced, trying out the words on her tongue. And she gave a radiant smile.